Mel, come on!"

"I'm coming." She strode across the dining room's hardwood floor and smiled at her sister's enthusiasm.

Bonnie took several impatient steps toward her, looped her arm around Melody's, and propelled her into the living room.

Seconds later, Melody came face-to-face with her sister's heartthrob.

Disbelief rocked her as she took in the man's reddish-brown hair, teal-green eyes, roughish grin, and broad shoulders.

No, it can't be!

ANDREA BOESHAAR was born and raised in Milwaukee, Wisconsin. Married for over twenty-seven years, she and her husband Daniel have three adult sons, two of whom are married. Andrea has been writing for more than twenty years, but writing exclusively for the Christian market for fifteen. Writing is something she loves to share, as well as, help others develop. Andrea is one of the cofounders of American Christian Fiction Writers and serves on the organization's advisory board.

HEARTSONG PRESENTS

Books under the pen name Andrea Shaar
HP079—An Unwilling Warrior

Books by Andrea Boeshaar
HP428—An Unmasked Heart
HP188—An Uncertain Heart
HP466—Risa's Rainbow
HP238—Annie's Song
HP541—The Summer Girl
HP270—Promise Me Forever
HP582—The Long Ride Home
HP279—An Unexpected Love
HP301—Second Time Around
HP342—The Haven of Rest
HP359—An Undaunted Faith
HP381—Southern Sympathies
HP401—Castle in the Clouds

Don't miss out on any of our super romances. Write to us at the following address for information on our newest releases and club information.

Heartsong Presents Readers' Service
PO Box 721
Uhrichsville, OH 44683

Or visit www.heartsongpresents.com

Always a Bridesmaid

Andrea Boeshaar

Heartsong Presents

To Sally, Nancy, Jeri, Christine, and Tamela—my Red Pen Club buddies. Thanks for your comments and suggestions. . . and especially for cheering me on as I wrote this book!

A note from the Author:
I love to hear from my readers! You may correspond with me by writing:

Andrea Boeshaar
Author Relations
PO Box 721
Uhrichsville, OH 44683

ISBN 1-59310-946-6

ALWAYS A BRIDESMAID

All scripture quotations, unless otherwise indicated, are taken from the HOLY BIBLE, NEW INTERNATIONAL VERSION®. NIV®. Copyright © 1973, 1978, 1984 by International Bible Society. Used by permission of Zondervan. All rights reserved.

All of the characters and events in this book are fictitious. Any resemblance to actual persons, living or dead, or to actual events is purely coincidental.

Our mission is to publish and distribute inspirational products offering exceptional value and biblical encouragement to the masses.

PRINTED IN THE U.S.A.

one

The news of her younger sister's engagement hit Melody Cartwright like a thick slab of icing off the side of an expensive wedding cake.

"Y—you're getting married?" She could hardly make the words form on her tongue.

Bonnie nodded while sheer delight heightened her lovely pale features. "Isn't it great?"

"But you just met the guy."

"Two months ago," Bonnie countered. "I wouldn't say I 'just' met him."

Mel considered her half sister. Even with her blond hair tousled and wearing an oversized red and white baseball jersey, Bonnie made a fetching sight. From her huge blue eyes and pert little nose to her tanned, slender legs and polished toenails—any man with eyes in his head could see she was a cute little package. No big surprise that Bonnie had gotten herself engaged.

But to whom? Mel shook her head. They knew nothing about this guy!

"A wedding to plan," their mother, Ellen Stenson, said on a dreamy note. She clasped her hands together. "This will be so much fun."

"Oh, won't it, though?"

Mel took in the gleeful expressions on Bonnie's and Mom's faces. They were so alike. Mom was Hollywood gorgeous, too, and typically became absorbed in Bonnie's pie-in-the-sky ideas.

"Aren't we jumpin' the gun a little bit here?" Dad asked. He sat in one of the matching armchairs on this sunny Saturday morning, attempting to read his newspaper.

"You're right, Bill. First things first." Slipping her arm around Bonnie's elbow, Mom guided her to the red, beige, and blue plaid sofa where they both sat down. "Tell us how you two met."

"I met him at work. He's a med student." She blushed. "Actually—I helped push through his application and he got accepted. He'll start this fall. Meanwhile, he's working part-time as a nursing assistant."

"Nursing is women's work, isn't it?" Dad remarked, peeking over the top of the sports section.

The ignorance of his remark caused Mel to grin in spite of the fact that he meant no insult. She knew her stepfather well. After all, he was the only dad she'd ever known. Her biological father had been killed during a routine Air Force training maneuver shortly after Mel's birth. Within a year, Mom had met and married Bill Stenson, a steely construction worker with a cushy heart. Eighteen months later, Bonnie was born.

However, this current scenario seemed a tad unfair to Melody. How could it be that her younger sister would get married before she would? That was Mel's dream—to be loved, honored, and cherished. But lately, with all her friends making their way to the altar, Mel was a bridesmaid over and over again; but never the bride.

And now Bonnie. . .

Lord, please quell this envy in my soul!

"Dad, being a nursing assistant isn't 'women's work,'" Bonnie argued. "It's hard work and preparation for becoming a *doctor*."

"Humph." Dad raised his newspaper a little higher and only the bald patch on his head was visible from Mel's vantage point.

"We have lunch together every day," Bonnie said, beaming. "We meet in the cafeteria."

"How—romantic." Mom pushed out a smile.

Mel folded her arms, wondering who paid. After all, a part-time nursing assistant wouldn't earn a lot of income. Melody worked a full-time job as a dental receptionist who, at times, assisted the hygienists. She didn't earn a whole lot of money and felt grateful her parents allowed her to live with them until she finished college via the Internet courses she took—or until she got married, the latter being Mel's preference. But, if she weren't living at home, she didn't know how she'd afford rent, car payments, gasoline, her cell phone, utilities, ongoing college expenses plus her student loans—and romantic cafeteria lunches.

"He's so wonderful," Bonnie gushed. "He's handsome and kind and—"

"Let's see your ring," Mel said, determined to shake off her misgivings and be happy for her sister.

"Oh. Well—I don't have a ring yet." Bonnie wiggled her bare left ring finger. "I have to pick it out at the jewelers."

"Hmm. Well, did he give you something else, like a locket or a bracelet?"

"When did you get so materialistic?" Bonnie charged. "No, he didn't give me anything, but I love *him*, not inanimate objects."

"No offense intended, Bon-bon," Mel said, using her little sister's nickname. "I just thought that maybe he gave you. . ." Melody looked from Mom to Dad and realized they wanted to hear the answer to this question, also. "I just thought he'd given you a token of his love and commitment."

"It's coming." Bonnie relaxed as a wistful smile curved her pink lips. "I'm so in love."

Mel didn't like the sound of this already. It seemed too fly-by-night. Too fast. Choosing one's spouse needed to be done with great care. Melody had learned that fact the hard way.

She'd known a guy in college who was bound for medical school. Scott Ramsay. She'd never forget him. Back then, Mel had thought he was Mr. Right, but he'd turned out to be Mr. All-Wrong! While she'd fallen in love with him, Scott had been dating half the female population on campus. That experience—while it took place more than three years ago—had been devastating. What's more, it had taught Melody to be very wary of whirlwind relationships where the opposite sex and her heart were concerned.

The big sister in her wanted to spare Bonnie the same anguish.

"Did it—um—ever occur to you that this guy might be using you, Bon-bon? He could be an opportunist looking forward to you putting him through med school."

"Good point," Dad said.

Melody found the gumption to continue. "Bonnie, think about it. You work at the medical college as the dean's administrative assistant, which means you've got connections. You already got him accepted—"

"No! That's not how it is." Bonnie stood and her sapphire eyes flashed with anger. "Why can't anyone be happy for me? Why is everyone being so negative?"

Dad lowered his newspaper to his lap. It lay there in a wrinkled heap. "Oh, now, don't start crying, Bonnie. I can't stand it when you girls cry."

Mom stood. "Bonnie, we're all—happy for you. It's just—well, such a shock. You haven't mentioned this young man before this morning." Mom's forehead wrinkled in a frown. "He is *young*, isn't he?"

"Of course he is!" Bonnie stamped her foot. "Do you think I'd marry some old geezer?"

"Watch it there, girly," Dad warned with a teasing gleam in his hazel eyes. "You're treading on thin ice."

Melody laughed and the atmosphere in the room changed at once.

Wearing a hint of a smile, Bonnie sat back down on the sofa. Mom did the same. Then, as Bonnie began babbling away about her fiancé, Mel walked to the kitchen and poured a cup of coffee. All the while she half listened to the conversation taking place in the living room.

"You didn't even tell us you were dating," Mom said. "Now suddenly you're—engaged?"

"Well, I didn't really know I was dating, either. But then. . . It just happened. We knew we were," she said, pausing dramatically, "*in love.*"

Mel sipped her coffee as her father strode into the room. Reaching around her, he grabbed a mug from the cupboard.

"This is like a bad soap opera," he groused.

"For sure." Melody grinned. She'd always appreciated her dad's sense of humor—even during the tough times.

"And just wait until I get my hands on this guy. Imagine asking my daughter to marry him when he doesn't even talk to me first! I mean—I haven't even met him."

"Right. And I'm sure you'd want to meet his folks, too. What if he was raised by an ax murderer or something?"

Deep creases appeared on Dad's brow. "Oh, no; I never thought of that!"

"Dad, I'm kidding." Mel laughed before taking a drink of coffee. She loved to tease her stepfather—and he teased her right back. "I'm sure this dude's parents are nice people."

"We'll see, won't we?" He shook his balding head. "And what about his faith? I just hope he's a believer!"

A moment later, Mom appeared at the doorway of the sunny yellow kitchen. Her eyes were wide and a tight smile tugged at her lips. The expression on her face said she'd overheard their conversation. "According to Bonnie, he's a believer. And guess what, Bill? God's granted your wish. Your youngest daughter's beloved will be here in less than an hour!"

"What!" Dad set down his coffee mug with a pronounced *thunk* before moaning his displeasure. "Saturday mornings are for leisure, family-only time!"

"I know, I know." Mom stepped into the kitchen, her hands

raised palms up as if to quell further argument. "But we have to meet him sooner or later. And as serious as Bonnie is about this man, I'd say the sooner the better!" She paused, before adding, "Besides, weddings take a long time to plan."

Mel deposited her coffee mug on the counter beside Dad's. She had to shower and dress; she still wore her cotton pink and white pajamas.

Mom sighed. "Good thing I cleaned the house yesterday." She tossed a glance at Mel. "I get first dibs on the bathroom."

"Go for it." Mel smiled in spite of the profound sense of foreboding gnawing at the pit of her stomach.

※

Some ninety minutes later, Melody stood in the large upstairs bedroom she shared with Bonnie. Her family lived in a typical Milwaukee, Wisconsin, bungalow; it had two bedrooms downstairs along with the living room, dining room, kitchen, and one bathroom. Mel and Bonnie's bedroom had once been a walk-up attic until Dad refinished it and the adjoining stairwell. Now the sisters shared a feminine peach-colored suite that included two half-wall partitions that gave them a semblance of privacy. However, Dad hadn't the foresight to build another bathroom.

After dressing in blue jeans and a yellow cotton short-sleeve shirt, Mel stood in front of the closet mirror and brushed out her short, light brown hair that was just long enough on the sides to tuck behind her ears. She could hear voices wafting up from downstairs: Bonnie's laugh and Dad's baritone as he spoke to Bonnie's intended.

I can't believe Mom and Dad are going to allow Bonnie to marry someone they never met and Bonnie only casually dated—if you can even call meeting in the cafeteria for lunch "dating."

The situation brought a sigh to Mel's lips. Weddings. She'd be a bridesmaid for the umpteenth time in June when her friends Darla and Max got married. Mel grew up with Max, but Darla only recently moved to the area; however, they were all a part of the career group at church.

And then Bonnie's wedding, whenever that date would be—Mel would most likely stand up at her younger sister's special ceremony.

Always a bridesmaid and never a bride. Lord, it just doesn't seem fair!

Melody crossed the room and stepped out onto the railed wooden platform. The city had required that another exit route be built for the attic bedroom, so Dad complied and added on this small porch overlooking the backyard.

She gazed upward. The sun warmed her face and neck. Temperatures were unseasonably warm for late April, and after last week's rain, the clear, azure skies were a welcome reprieve.

Lord, please take away my jealousy over Bonnie getting married. Mel gazed heavenward then closed her eyes. *Please help me to be happy for her. I would want her to be happy for me if I were getting married. And on that subject, Lord, I just wondered—*

"Hi, Melody!"

Her prayers interrupted, she looked down and saw Luke Berringer lift his hand in a quick wave.

She waved back. Luke had been her next-door neighbor ever since Mel could remember. They'd gone through elementary school and high school together and attended the same church. Luke was as familiar a fixture in Melody's life as the chestnut tree in her backyard—and she gave Luke just about as much thought.

"Are you going bowling this afternoon with the career group? We're going out to eat afterward."

"No. Can't go." Mel had actually forgotten all about the outing. "We're having company. In fact, I think he's arrived. I need to get myself downstairs. See ya later."

She waved again and then before Luke could say another thing, she reentered the bedroom. After giving her hair another good brushing and a shot of hair spray, she prayerfully descended the steps into the back hallway just off the kitchen and headed for the living room to meet her younger sister's fiancé.

❧

That woman is really bad for my ego, Luke thought as he resumed raking his yard.

He blew out a frustrated breath. He'd been infatuated with Melody Cartwright since the fourth grade, but she barely knew he existed. During high school he'd been too shy to ask her out, not that his parents would have allowed it. His folks, both now in heaven with Jesus, believed dating was a prelude to marriage and not the "sport" society made it out to be. Luke had adhered to their wishes. He didn't date in high school, but in the years that followed, he dated here and there, although he hadn't found a woman who captured his full range of emotions like Melody had. He admired her tenacity, her wit, her lovely smile—and, *wow*, could that woman sing! She lived up to her name, that's for sure, except he hadn't heard her sing in a long while. She'd dropped out of the choir at church when she came home from college a few years ago. Nevertheless, Luke sensed her deep faith. As for looks, Melody was about the prettiest girl he knew, but pretty in a wholesome way—one his mother had approved of. Mom had always adored "Mellie," and now Luke would sure like to date her—and in his parents' sense of the word. He was no longer a shy and reclusive boy, and at twenty-six years old he'd already forged out a successful career for himself as a real estate agent. He'd purchased the house he'd been raised in, and he couldn't help thinking about a wife and family as he roamed around the large rooms.

Luke raked out a pile of muck from underneath the evergreen bushes. They grew along the chain-link fence separating the Stensons' yard from his. So how did he get Melody to take notice of him? Luke hadn't a clue. He'd tried just about everything except a bullhorn. Even Dan Rebholtz, the pastor overseeing the career group at church, had commented on Luke's interest in Melody. Several of his friends knew about it, too. Why was it obvious to others, but not her?

Well, maybe it wasn't meant to be. Luke tried to keep an open mind. He wanted God's will for his life, after all.

He just wanted Melody to be a part of it.

two

Mel, come on!"

"I'm coming." She strode across the dining room's hardwood floor and smiled at her sister's enthusiasm.

Bonnie took several impatient steps toward her, looped her arm around Melody's, and propelled her into the living room.

Seconds later, Melody came face-to-face with her sister's heartthrob.

Disbelief rocked her as she took in the man's reddish-brown hair, teal-green eyes, roughish grin, and broad shoulders.

No, it can't be!

"Mel, I want you to meet Scott Ramsay," Bonnie said in a girlish tone. "Scott, this is my sister, Melody Cartwright."

Recognition flashed in his eyes, but he didn't acknowledge it. "Nice to meet you."

He extended his right hand, although Mel didn't take it. Hurt, anger, betrayal, envy—practically every emotion known to mankind pumped through her veins. Her face flamed with all she felt inside.

"Actually, we've already met." Melody's tone was sharper than she intended, so she made a concerted effort to soften it. "Yeah," she said, ignoring Scott's look of chagrin, "we met at college, the University of Madison. We were part of SFC, Students for Christ." Melody tipped her head, surprised and hurt by the blank expression on Scott's face.

"Um—yeah, I participated in SFC, but. . ." He narrowed his gaze as though struggling to remember her. "What's your name again?"

Mel figured his question was intended to maim—and it did.

It gouged open a three-and-a-half-year-old wound.

Years ago, Scott had said he loved her on more than one occasion. He'd whispered her name in the most intimate of ways. How could he forget?

Then again, he'd had a virtual harem on campus. Scott put King Solomon to shame—before he vanished, that is.

Mel had searched high and low for him, fearing something terrible had happened. But what she found were other women looking for Scott, too—and one was pregnant. Ginger Atavack. Feeling helpless and alone, the young woman chose to have an abortion in spite of Melody's attempts to talk her out of it.

"Mel and I are half sisters," Bonnie said. She'd obviously sensed that Melody was at a loss for words. "Her last name is different because she's the only Cartwright grandchild and Mom promised Mel's grandmother she wouldn't change it. My last name is. . . Well, you know—my last name." Bonnie giggled, evidently embarrassed by her uncharacteristic babbling.

Scott tore his gaze from Mel and bestowed a handsome smile on her younger sister. It was a smile she remembered well.

Melody felt sick.

"Well, it's great that you've met Scott already, sweetie pie," Mom said, wearing an odd expression.

Glancing at her mother, Melody sensed she'd have some explaining to do later. But for now, she'd have to hide behind a polite facade.

"Well, let's all sit down and eat." Dad held out his hand, indicating the dining room table. "Don't know about all of you, but I'm starved."

Mel took a seat across the table from Bonnie and Scott. Throughout their lunch, which consisted of hard rolls and deli-sliced cold cuts and cheese, Melody kept her gaze as far from Scott as possible. It was just a good thing she liked to eat when she felt stressed or she might have seemed rude and called further attention to herself. She didn't want her family to think she was jealous of Bonnie—even though she was, to a degree—and she'd never told her parents about Scott, although she'd meant to. But between classes, homework, her involvement in SFC, and making time to see him, she'd never gotten the chance. She had dreamed of bringing him home during spring break. However, by then, Scott had disappeared.

With their meal finished, Melody jumped up and offered to clear the table and wash dishes.

"Well, thanks, honey." Mom smiled. "Now I can spend time getting to know Scott."

A grateful gleam shone in Bonnie's blue eyes.

"Hey, no problem." Melody carried plates into the kitchen. Little did her family know that she wouldn't have sat in the living room and chatted with Scott Ramsay if her life depended on it. The more she remembered about him, the more she felt hatred worming its way into her heart.

Lord, help me. I'm feeling anything but Christlike at the moment.

Mel battled her emotions and focused on the tasks at hand: putting away leftovers and loading the dishwasher. She wondered what she should do about Scott. How would she tell her parents? And what about Bonnie? Melody knew her sister was crazy about the guy.

So was I—once.

At the sound of a man clearing his voice, Mel whirled around and found the object of her tumultuous thoughts standing in the kitchen's entrance.

"What can I do for you, Scott? Want another cola?"

Shaking his head, he stepped forward and Mel willed herself to stay calm.

"I remember you. It's coming back to me now. We were friends, but I can tell you don't feel that way about me anymore.

In fact, I'd say you dislike me."

"Friends?" Melody blinked. "Is that what you call it?"

"Sure." Scott paused and then a look of pity crossed his features. "Oh, I get it. You thought our relationship was something more, huh? That's too bad."

Melody clamped her jaw shut and glanced away from Scott's condescending stare.

"Look, I know I said and did some things in Madison that I shouldn't have. Those were wild days for me, but I'm a changed man."

"Yeah, that has yet to be determined."

He raised his hands in a helpless gesture.

"Scott?"

At the sound of Bonnie's voice, he pivoted, and Melody glanced at the doorway. Dressed in a denim skirt and pink V-neck sweater that heightened her rosy complexion, it wasn't hard to see why Scott or any other man would be attracted to Bonnie.

And Melody felt it was her duty to protect her sister. She had a feeling Scott Ramsay hadn't changed all that much. But how did she sound the warning without appearing like a jealous, green monster?

"I've been waiting for you, Scott." Bonnie sent him an uncertain smile. "Thought you got lost."

"Well, he does have a knack for disappearing," Melody mumbled under her breath.

Scott laughed it off. "Melody and I were reminiscing about our college days. We sure had some fun times in Madison, didn't we?" He nudged her with his elbow.

Melody wanted to sock him. How dare he make light of the worst time in her life! Because of Scott's "wild" days on the UWM campus, Melody's life would never be the same.

Neither would the lives of several other young women.

"So—um—did you end up graduating?" Scott ventured

casually. His gaze rested on Melody.

She shook her head, deciding she'd rather die before admitting that he was the reason she didn't return to school.

"But she's taking correspondence courses," Bonnie offered. "She's close to earning her degree in English, right, Mel?"

"Right."

"I thought you were a music major."

"You remember that much, do you?" Mel slid her gaze to Scott.

A look of chagrin crossed his ruddy features. "Yep, it's all coming back to me."

"Mel decided she can do more with an English degree," Bonnie said. Confusion puckered her winged brows as she gazed from Scott to Mel.

Melody smiled at her sister. Bonnie had earned her degree in professional communications and business management in less than four years. Melody always found it amazing that for a woman with little to no common sense, Bonnie was really quite brilliant.

"What do you say we rejoin Mom and Dad in the living room?" Bonnie held out her hand to Scott. "I know they want to hear more about you."

Scott took it and the two strolled toward the doorway.

Bonnie glanced over her shoulder. "Coming, Mel?"

"No, I—um—I've got to go—somewhere."

"Oh, yeah, today's the bowling outing with the career group."

Before Melody could answer, Bonnie had disappeared with Scott into the next room.

Mel sagged against the sink. She felt emotionally bruised from her exchange with Scott and feared more of the same would occur in the future. She had to do something. But what?

Deciding a drive would clear her head and get her out of

the house, Mel ran upstairs, grabbed her purse, and then made her way outside and across the backyard to the carport. In this particular neighborhood, there were no driveways in front of or alongside the homes; instead, the garages were built just off the alleyway running parallel to the rear property line. The Stensons were fortunate to have a two-car garage, and Dad had built the carport for Mel's and Bonnie's vehicles. Both their cars fit inside the open-ended structure, but with little room to spare. Still, it lent some protection against the harsh Wisconsin winters.

Climbing into her yellow Cavalier coupe, Melody stuck the key into the ignition and fired up the engine. She considered the career group outing, but she didn't feel like bowling, and she certainly didn't want to answer questions about Bonnie's new beau! Before Scott arrived, Bonnie had telephoned at least a dozen of her friends and announced she was getting married.

Lord, why is this happening?

Putting the car into gear, Mel backed out of the carport into the alley, concentrating on keeping enough distance between her vehicle and Bonnie's little red SRT; however, in doing so Mel failed to look behind her—

Until it was too late.

three

Melody, are you hurt?"

Dazed, she blinked before staring up at the man holding open her car door. His light brown eyes were wide with concern; then the rest of his features came into focus.

"Luke!"

"I couldn't stop in time. I'm sorry. Are you all right?"

Melody shifted the lever into park, wiggled her toes, flexed her fingers, and did a few neck rolls. "I think I'm fine. Just a little shaken."

Luke extended his hand and helped Melody from the car. "Doesn't seem to be any damage to my vehicle, but your rear quarter panel got pretty smashed."

Melody gaped at the huge dent in the left side of her car. Although Luke couldn't have been going more than fifteen miles per hour, the collision had swung her vehicle forty-five degrees. Her Cavalier now faced one end of the alley and Luke's black Durango faced the other.

"Like I said, I couldn't stop in time."

"I—it was my fault," she stammered. "I should have looked before backing into the alley. But I was so worried about scratching Bonnie's car that I forgot to check for oncoming traffic."

Luke didn't reply but bent at the waist to give the damage on her car a closer inspection. Next he rechecked his SUV.

Melody thought about how she'd have to call her insurance agent on Monday. She had a five-hundred-dollar deductible, which meant she'd be forced to dip into her savings. Her goal was to have twenty thousand dollars in the bank by the time she got married so she could have the wedding she always wanted. She'd already selected her wedding gown, her colors—deep blue and gold—and she knew exactly where she'd hold her reception. All she needed was the groom and about fifteen thousand more dollars. Mel stared at her car. Another setback. Another dagger—tearing her dreams to shreds.

Unfortunately, in her imaginings about her wedding day, Melody had always pictured a man who looked very much like Scott Ramsay—Mr. All-Wrong—at her side. It was a disconcerting image.

Then she recalled all his empty promises to her and other women years ago, and now his adoring looks at Bonnie this afternoon.

What a jerk!

"Melody?"

She snapped from her musings and wiped an errant tear off her cheek. She hoped Luke hadn't seen the gesture.

"I think your whole back bumper is going to have to be replaced," he told her, wearing an expression of remorse. "Your Cavalier was no match for my Durango, I'm afraid." He paused. "Hey, are you all right?"

Melody couldn't contain the onslaught of emotion. It had already been a trying day and this ill-fated fender bender just topped it off. Thankfully, it hadn't been a noisy accident. The last thing she needed was her family and Scott out here, gawking and asking questions.

Luke stepped closer, and Melody got a whiff of his spicy, woodsy cologne. "Don't cry. Do you have car insurance?"

She nodded.

He set his hand on her shoulder. "Tell you what—I'll pay half of your deductible. Will that help?"

"That's not necessary," she eked out. Oddly, his benevolence only made her tears flow all the more. "It's just been a bad day."

"Want me to get your dad?"

"No!"

At Luke's wide-eyed gaze, Melody felt the need to explain her exclamatory reply. Besides, Luke would probably hear about Bonnie's engagement soon enough.

"My parents have company. You see. . ." Melody sniffed. "This morning Bonnie announced she's getting married."

"No kidding?" Luke brought his chin back. "To whom?"

"No one you know. Bonnie met the guy at work. Except, here's the thing—I knew him in college."

"At UWM? In Madison?"

Mel bobbed out a reply, feeling a little surprised that Luke remembered which university she'd attended. "His name is Scott and, well—I sort of—dated him," she added, brushing the last of her tears away. A renewed burst of resentment caused her to clench her fists before she shoved them into the pockets of her jeans. "And now he's marrying Bonnie."

Melody gazed at her dented automobile while she spoke. But when Luke didn't reply, she glanced back at him. He looked like someone had just punched him in the gut.

Melody blinked. "What's wrong?"

Luke seemed to shake himself. "Um—nothing."

He shifted, appearing uncomfortable, and Mel wondered what she'd said to put him at such unease.

"Well—um—if you're okay, I guess I'll be going."

"Oh, right. The career group outing." She waved her hand at him. "I'm fine. Sorry to have held you up this long."

Luke replied with a slight nod and then climbed into his SUV, leaving Melody with the distinct impression that she'd offended him.

As she slipped into the driver's seat of her car, she mentally went over everything she told Luke and couldn't fathom that any of her words would cause the slightest offense.

Unless Luke was interested in Bonnie.

Mel considered the notion as she started her engine and

backed up. A sharp scraping noise caused her to slam on the brakes and grimace. Apparently, she wasn't driving anywhere now.

Moments later, Luke's SUV reappeared. Melody realized he'd gone around the block and driven back into the alley. He passed his driveway, pulled up beside her, and stopped. He rolled down his window and Mel did the same.

"Let's go have a cup of coffee."

"What?" Mel found it a strange offer.

"You're obviously upset and—well, I'm a friend. We've known each other forever. I—I just want to be there for you."

Melody was touched by his kindness. "That's nice, Luke." She even managed a smile. "But—"

"I don't feel like bowling anyhow."

Mel looked at her steering wheel and thought it over. "I have to get my car back into the carport until my dad can look at it."

"I'll help you. You drive, I'll push."

Melody opened her mouth to protest, but before she could utter a single sound, Luke pulled forward and parked. Then he hopped out of his SUV.

Melody relented; it didn't appear he'd take no for an answer anyhow. Besides, having coffee with Luke would kill some time, and it sure beat hanging around the house with Scott Ramsay all afternoon.

❧

Luke willed his heart to stop hammering as he pushed Melody's vehicle into the carport. Was it jealousy or anxiety pumping through his veins?

Melody parked and killed the engine. Luke walked back to his Durango and slid behind the wheel. He hadn't meant to come off as pushy, but as a real estate agent he'd learned how to propel people toward making decisions—especially when they wavered, as Melody had done moments ago. Had he left it up to her, she wouldn't be climbing into his SUV right now. But he couldn't let this opportunity escape him. This was his chance to be her hero—the moment he'd been waiting for since grade school!

Lord, help me not to react negatively to anything she might tell me about that guy she dated in Madison.

Luke clenched his jaw, but then forced himself to relax. What did he expect? Melody was a lovely young lady with a matching personality. Of course she'd date. But what did that word really signify? Dinner at the pizza parlor a few times or something much more?

Luke sensed it was the latter or Melody wouldn't be so upset that the guy was marrying Bonnie.

He shook off his troubled thoughts and waited until Melody strapped on the seat belt before he drove to the end of the alley and made a right.

"It's a nice day. Want to go to that new coffeehouse on the east side, by the lake?"

"The farther away the better." There was an edge to her voice.

"I take it you're not pleased that Bonnie's marrying this guy. What did you say his name is? Scott?" Luke cleared his throat. "Is it because you still have feelings for him?"

"Which question do you want answered first?"

Luke raised his brows, feeling a tad insulted by her tone. But in the next moment, she apologized.

"I'm sorry, Luke. I don't mean to take it out on you. I'm just really upset and angry. I thought I was over Scott. I thought I didn't feel anything for him anymore, but then seeing him today brought back all the hurt I felt when he dumped me. Actually, I think it's more about the humiliation I still feel than anything else. And he was so arrogant today. Not a single word of remorse or regret. He's just a complete jerk, and I can't believe Bonnie's going to marry him!"

Luke felt like maybe he'd gotten in over his head. He sent up a quick prayer for wisdom. He didn't have much experience with "upset and angry" females. They scared him to death.

But this was different. Melody was a sister in Christ, his next-door neighbor, and the girl of his dreams. The way Luke saw it, no pain no gain.

"So—um—how'd you meet Scott?"

"We met at one of the on-campus meetings for Students for Christ. Ooh, was I stupid. I didn't recognize a danger sign when it stared me in the face. I mean, talk about a wolf in sheep's clothing!"

The dam broke, and as he drove the next fifteen miles, Luke listened to Melody pour out her heart. In a way, Luke felt privileged to be her confidant, but he also had to force himself to watch the road and pretend that none of what she said hurt his feelings.

"So, as far as I was concerned," she prattled on, "we were in love. But then Scott disappeared off the face of the earth. That's when I discovered he'd been dating half the women on campus—and one woman was carrying his child, but she terminated her pregnancy. I tried to counsel her, but it didn't help. It was a very traumatic time in my life. I felt like such a failure both emotionally and spiritually."

"I can imagine," Luke said, parking his vehicle in the coffee-house's crowded lot.

"Then this morning, Scott shows up in family's living room, engaged to Bonnie!" Melody released her seat belt. "What's more, he corners me in the kitchen to tell me he's a changed man. But he never apologized for anything. He just made excuses. He referred to his experience in Madison as his 'wild days,' and he termed our relationship as 'just friends.'" Melody expelled an audible, exasperated breath. "Oooooh! What a rat!"

Luke felt like he had twenty daggers protruding from his

chest as he walked alongside Melody to the coffeehouse. But he reminded himself the pain would be worth it if he could get closer to Melody.

ঽ

Melody was awed by her surroundings as they entered the cream city brick building. Milwaukee was not only famous for its beer manufacturing in the late 1800s, but for a certain type of clay found along the shores of Lake Michigan that, after being fired, turned a buttery color, earning the name "Cream City brick." The coffeehouse, originally a pumping station, had been constructed of the strong brick and recently underwent a face-lift after the coffee company purchased it from the city. Melody heard about this place, drove past it, and even read about it in the newspaper after it opened, but she hadn't actually been inside. What impressed her most about this coffeehouse/deli was that, although renovated, much of the structure's charm still remained, from the lofted ceiling with its brightly painted piping to the unpainted brick walls and plank floor. Mel was something of a history buff with a penchant for old buildings, and this one certainly filled her senses.

But at the moment, the coffeehouse was packed, so after purchasing flavored brews, Melody and Luke decided on a walk along the lakefront. The breeze off Lake Michigan felt cool, but the sun was warm.

"Did that ever happen to you?" Mel prompted.

Luke glanced at her before sipping his coffee. "Did what ever happen?"

"You know, falling for someone only to find out she didn't feel the same about you—or she cheated on you."

"Well, not in that way, but—um—yeah, I guess it has happened to me." Luke paused and seemed to collect his thoughts. "I'm crazy about someone who barely knows I exist."

Mel found the information fascinating. "You are?"

Luke nodded. "Uh-huh."

"Who is she?"

"I'd rather not say." A sheepish expression crossed his face. "I'd feel kinda stupid if the news got out."

"But that's just it, Luke. You have to let the news out. How else is this person supposed to know you're interested in her?"

He shrugged and sipped his coffee. "I'd like the Holy Spirit to let her know."

"Yeah, I guess you're right." Melody thought God's way was always the best, and she chided herself for being so impatient. And curious. "So, do I know her?"

"Yep, you sure do."

Melody knew at once who this mystery girl was: Bonnie! *So my hunch was right!*

They walked awhile longer, then sat down on a park bench that faced the lagoon. In the distance, the Milwaukee Art Museum's modern structure, created by Santiago Calatrava, spread its wings toward Lake Michigan.

Melody pulled one leg up so her left foot rested on the bench and then wrapped her arm around her knee. In the other hand, she held her coffee. She didn't say a word and neither did Luke, and Melody was amazed at the amicable silence that settled quite naturally between them.

Except the silence made her wonder what Luke was thinking. She'd mentioned Ginger and the abortion. . . .

"Luke, just for the record," she began, "I never slept with Scott."

The poor guy almost choked on his last gulp of coffee.

Melody laughed at his reaction, clapping his back between his shoulder blades.

Hunched over and wiping dribbles of coffee from his chin, he glanced at her. "The thought never entered my head."

"I'm glad." Relief washed over her. "But I felt I had to say something and put all doubts to rest here and now. I mean, you and I attend the same church, and we're part of the same career group—I don't want you to think I'm a hypocrite."

"You know what, Melody? I've always been amazed at your ability to say what's on your mind."

She lifted her shoulders. "Bad habit."

Luke grinned, sat back, and extended his arm along the bench's backrest. "Look, *just for the record*," he said, quoting her, "I'd never think the worst about you. I only think the best of you."

His words stirred Melody in an odd way, and she noted it was the second tender thing he'd told her today.

Then suddenly Mel looked at him—*really* looked at him. Perhaps for the first time in years. Luke Berringer had always been that shy, dorky boy next door. But today he seemed anything *but* dorky. His short, straight, dark brown hair was combed back in a style that was longer on top and shorter around the sides and back. Dark, rectangular wire-framed glasses complemented his honey-colored eyes. A handsome guy, according to Mel's appraisal. When had that happened?

Her gaze traveled downward, and she noticed Luke possessed a strong jawline, a muscular neck—a telltale sign that he habitually worked out, maybe lifted weights. His broad shoulders strained against the fabric of his mossy-green polo shirt.

Melody quickly glanced away. What did she think she was doing, gawking at Luke that way! What was her problem?

She stared out over the lagoon where ducks swam in its murky depths. But it soon became apparent that Luke might become just the friend she needed right now—the one who'd be able to relate to what she was going through. After all, if he had planned to pursue Bonnie, he'd had his dreams dashed today, too.

"Luke, I think we have a lot in common," she muttered before taking a sip of coffee.

"I think you're right."

Melody turned and regarded him once more. She noted the hint of a grin that tugged at his mouth.

She smiled. "Guess I'm glad I *ran into you* today."

At that, they both laughed.

four

Melody couldn't say for sure how it happened, but at supper-time, she found herself at a restaurant with Luke and the rest of the career group from church. Maybe it was the fact that Luke was driving combined with the reality that Melody didn't want to go home for fear Scott Ramsay was still there. But whatever the case, Mel decided to relax and have a good time with her friends. She'd taken Luke's advice, and when asked about Bonnie's sudden engagement, she merely stated it wasn't for her to discuss; they'd have to talk with Bonnie about it.

"Oh, come on," Wendy Tomlinson prodded. Her green eyes lit with curiosity and her long, light brown hair hung in curls around her sweet, round face. "You can at least toss us a morsel. Is he nice? Good-looking?"

With all eyes on her now, Melody didn't know how reply. Of course Scott was handsome, not to mention charming. And Mel recalled how years ago he could make her knees weak with a simple glance in her direction.

But, nice? Hardly! A rogue and a scoundrel? Definitely! Of course, Mel couldn't give such a description of her younger sister's fiancé.

"Scott's okay," she finally replied. She hoped she sounded flip and disinterested. "But we have better-looking guys right here in this career group."

The men at the table cheered like they were at a basketball game, turning heads all around the restaurant, and Melody laughed. Beside her, Luke chuckled, and soon the topic changed, much to Melody's relief.

"Hey, Luke, how's the home selling business going?" Mike Johnson asked. He leaned forward and the light above him gave his blond crew cut a funky, golden hue. Mike had joined up with the National Guard right after high school, so he'd been dubbed *Military Mike*. "Now that interest rates have gone up, no one's buying, eh?"

"On the contrary, I sold two—possibly three—houses this week." Luke grinned. "Great week for me."

"Sounds like it," Mike replied with a smirk. "But no one's buying electronics. Maybe I should get into real estate."

"I've only been telling you that for the last five years."

Everyone chuckled at the comeback and, for the second time that day, Melody scrutinized Luke Berringer. His dark hair had fallen into a casual, off-center part, and he reminded her of the lead actor in a movie her sociology class had been required to watch years ago.

So if he's Hollywood handsome, why isn't he married—or at least spoken for?

But then, Melody reasoned, if Luke had his heart set on Bonnie, he probably hadn't made himself available.

Melody mulled over the situation and wondered if she could somehow make Bonnie see that Luke was the better catch. Maybe then Scott would slither back under whatever rock he came from, and he'd leave her family alone.

With dinner long finished, members of the career group left one by one. Finally Melody and Luke were the only ones at the table.

"I don't feel like going home," she admitted, "but I don't want to keep you out if you need to be on your way." She sipped the cup of lukewarm decaf she'd been nursing for the past half hour.

Luke shook his head. "I don't have any pressing engagements."

"Thanks."

He grinned. "Sure."

Melody returned his smile. "So, tell me, do you like working in real estate? I sort of forgot that's what you did for a living."

Luke sat back in his chair. "Yeah, I enjoy it. I'm basically my own boss." He tipped his head. "Do you like working as a dental receptionist?"

Melody blinked in surprise. She couldn't believe he remembered her occupation. She figured he must have one of those incredible memories. "Actually, I hate my job, but I love the people I work with so that makes going to work every day tolerable."

"Why do you hate your job?" A frown pulled at Luke's dark brows.

Mel stared into her coffee. "Well, it was only supposed to be a temporary position. I had hoped to get married and have kids, but—"

"But things didn't work out with Scott Ramsay."

Melody tried to discern the edge in Luke's voice and finally attributed it to losing Bonnie to the creep.

"Just for the record, it 'didn't work out with Scott' long before I was hired at Dr. Leonard's dental office."

With a pitcher in each hand, the waitress paused at their table and refilled Melody's coffee and Luke's ice water. Then she scurried away.

"Actually, I have a lot of respect for domestic engineers," Luke said. "It's a noble profession. My sister—you remember Amber, right?"

"Of course." As Mel recalled, Amber was four years older than she and Luke.

"Well, Amber and her husband, Karl, have four children and whenever I visit them I'm reminded of what an awesome responsibility parenting is."

Mel agreed. "But I think it's a big turnoff for guys—you know, a woman who wants to be a stay-at-home mom. Men these days want a career wife, someone who can ease their financial responsibilities. At least that's been my experience."

"Do you date a lot?" Luke asked, lifting his glass and sucking an ice cube into his mouth.

"What's 'a lot'? I think I've had three dates in the past year. None went any further than a second date, and I met all three guys at my friends' weddings."

"Hmm. You've a better track record than I do. I'll bet I've had three dates in the last five years."

Mel shook her head at him. "What's up with that? You're a terrific guy. I'm surprised some woman hasn't snatched you up by now."

He shrugged and a sheepish expression spread across his face. "I must be dating all the career women."

Mel found the remark amusing. But then her smile faded, and she looked at him thoughtfully. Curiosity gnawed at her. "Is the real truth because you had your heart set on—on that woman you told me you're crazy about, only she barely knows you're alive?"

"Naw, I don't think so. I'm somewhat of an opportunist, and if the chance comes along to go out to dinner with a pretty lady who happens to be a Christian, I'll take it." Luke leaned closer to her. "In other words, I know better than to sit at home alone and pine away for someone." Sitting back, Luke took a deep breath. "But, you know, things are looking up."

"They are?" Mel couldn't help feeling a little conspiratorial. "You mean with this woman you're crazy about?"

Luke nodded.

"Was she here tonight?"

"Yep." The wry grin on his face grew into an embarrassed smile.

"She was!" *So it's not Bonnie after all.*

Melody thought about the women at the table. Wendy Tomlinson, Marlene Dorsche, Sarah Canterfield, Jamie Becker, and Alicia Sims. "Well, that narrows it down," she said smugly before pointing a finger at him. "I'm going to guess who this mystery girl is, Luke."

He laughed and pushed his chair back. "You do that." He stood and extended his hand, helping Melody to her feet. "This place is getting crowded and noisy. Let's get out of here."

≈

Since the night was still young, Luke pulled out his cell phone and called his buddy Tom Wheeler. He asked if he and Melody could stop by. Tom replied with an emphatic "yes" that Mel could hear from where she sat in the passenger seat of Luke's SUV.

"You'll like Tom and his wife, Emily," Luke told her as he drove to the Wheelers' home. "I've worked with Tom for years. He and Em are believers, and they were a big help to me after my parents died."

Mel digested the information. "It was tragic that you lost both your mom and dad so close to each other." She only vaguely recalled that time; she'd been away at school in Madison.

"Yeah, it was tough. Mom died of breast cancer, and Dad had a stroke shortly after. He went downhill from there."

Melody thought back on her childhood, remembering Mr. and Mrs. Berringer. "I always liked your folks."

Luke shot her a grin. "They liked you, too." He chuckled. "You amused them for hours with your pet rabbit in the backyard when you were a little girl. My parents talked about it years later."

"I was always trying to train my rabbit—I must have been eight or nine years old." Mel grinned at the memory. "All my life I've wanted a puppy, but my parents never let me have one because my mom has a lot of allergies. So I had to make do with Snowy the rabbit—and Snowy was never allowed in the house. During the wintertime, my third grade teacher kept Snowy in our classroom."

"Oh, sure, I remember Snowy and her glass-sided cage with

its metal screen top sitting in the back of the classroom." Luke chuckled.

Melody expelled a dramatic sigh. "Yeah, well, I never did get her to bark. She certainly wasn't the puppy I always wanted."

Luke laughed again, and Mel decided she enjoyed making him smile. She always remembered Luke as being a reticent kid. In his teens he was a geeky bookworm. But now he appeared every bit the handsome gentleman—but maybe still shy, if he didn't want to tell the woman who he was "crazy about" of his feelings.

Maybe I can help him along.

At last they arrived at the Wheelers' ranch-style house. The couple lived in the Village of Brown Deer, not too far from the urban neighborhood in which Luke and Mel resided.

"Please come in," Emily Wheeler beckoned as they reached the front door.

They entered the living room, and Mel noticed the modest furnishings. She also sensed the warmth and hominess of the place. Framed needlework graced the white walls and an autumn-colored knitted afghan covered the back of a beige, three-cushioned sofa.

Luke made the introductions.

"Nice to meet you," Emily Wheeler said.

"Same here." Mel gave her a smile while taking in the other woman's appearance. Tall and slender, Mel thought of her as plain at first. Her ash-blond hair hung straight nearly to her waist, although the top section had been secured in the back with a barrette. But moments later, Mel saw the sweetness in Emily's countenance and decided the woman was actually quite lovely.

"Have a seat," she urged.

At that moment, Tom entered the living room and pumped Luke's hand with enthusiasm. "Luke, buddy, I'm glad you dropped in."

Once more, Luke introduced Melody, and Tom shook her hand with an equal amount of exuberance.

"Are you two up for a game of Trivial Pursuit?" Tom cast an eager glance at Luke, then Melody.

Luke leaned over and muttered, "Tom's a TP nut."

"So am I!" Mel couldn't believe her good fortune. "What versions do you have?"

"All of them." Tom's grin lit up the living room. His height matched his wife's, but instead of being slender, he possessed a stocky frame. "What's your pleasure?"

"How 'bout the Know-It-All Edition?"

"You got it! What do you say we play guys against girls?"

"Well," Melody said with a wry grin, "only if Luke wants to lose."

Luke chuckled.

"Lose? Ha!" Tom lifted his chin. "I'm the champion at Trivial Pursuit."

"I don't know about that," Mel countered. "You may have just met your match."

"Ooooooh," Luke said, feigning in an ominous tone.

Mel elbowed him in the arm for the retort.

Emily laughed softly and lowered herself into a nearby armchair. Meanwhile, Tom left the room to get the board game, and Luke took a seat on the couch. Melody plopped down next to him.

"Hey, Em? Maybe you ought to put on a pot of coffee."

Emily's smile grew and she nodded. "I was thinking along the same lines, Luke. Between Tom and Melody going at it, this could prove to be a long night."

five

"I can't believe he's still here!"

Melody gazed out the passenger-side window as Luke pulled up to the curb in front of his house instead of driving into the alley out back where the garages were. Luke killed the engine and said he'd decided to keep his SUV on the street tonight. Parked just ahead of them, in front of her parents' house, sat Scott Ramsay's sleek, silver Pontiac Trans Am. Mel guessed, with little effort, that the sports car belonged to Scott because its license plate read: RAMSAM.

"So how does a part-time nursing assistant afford a Trans Am?"

"His great-aunt bought it for him?"

"What?" Mel turned and peered at Luke's shadowy figure.

He laughed, and she realized he was teasing.

"Well, whatever. It's after midnight," she lamented. "It's time for that man to *go home!*"

"If you want to forestall the inevitable some more, I suppose we could go get some ice cream or order a pizza."

Mel frowned at placed a hand over her stomach. "After all the munchies I ate at the Wheelers' tonight, I don't think I could swallow another crumb."

"Okay, just remember I offered."

Luke's quiet chuckle reached her ears, but before she could retort, he was out of the SUV. Walking around the vehicle, he opened her door and helped her out.

"I had a fun time today, Luke."

"Me, too. I especially enjoyed watching you and Tom spar over that Trivial Pursuit game."

Melody laughed. "Em and I let you guys win. You know that, right?"

"Right." There wasn't much conviction in Luke's tone.

"Well, thanks for everything."

"You're welcome."

"Good night."

"Not yet." Luke stepped beside her as Mel ambled to the front steps.

She glanced at him, surprised.

"I'm afraid the curiosity will keep me awake all night if I don't meet this guy—Scott."

"Really?"

They reached the door and under the soft glow of the porch light, Mel saw him nod.

"Good, then I won't have to walk in alone."

She stuck her key into the lock, turned the knob, and gave the heavy wooden door a bump with her hip. The door opened and Melody led Luke inside. They found her family—and Mr. All-Wrong—seated in the dining room. Paper and magazines were scattered across the table's polished surface.

"Oh, hi, Mel!" Bonnie extended her arm in a large wave. "How was bowling? Hi, Luke!"

He inclined his head. "Bonnie."

"We didn't go bowling," Mel said, setting her purse on the buffet. "But we met up with the career group for dinner."

"Oh, that's nice," her sister replied with distracted grin.

Realizing they had another guest, both Mom and Dad rose and greeted Luke.

"How've you been? I haven't seen you in half of forever."

Mel smiled as she watched her mother give Luke a hug.

"Luke, come over here and meet my fiancé," Bonnie interjected. "Honey, I want you to meet Luke Berringer. He's our next-door neighbor."

Honey? Mel tried to choke down her cynicism as the two men clasped hands. She decided it'd be interesting to hear Luke's first impressions. But in the next moment, she recognized the disarray on the table.

"Hey," she said, pointing to the opened magazines.

"Oh, I borrowed all your bridal magazines and catalogs," Bonnie explained. "I figured you wouldn't mind since I'll need them before you do."

Mel clamped her jaw shut.

"And look! I've already selected my colors. Navy blue and gold."

"What?" Melody felt like she'd been slapped.

"Navy blue and gold," Bonnie repeated, slower this time.

But those are my colors! Mel wanted to shout.

She compressed her jaw even tighter.

"The kids decided on a date," Mom informed both Melody and Luke. A gleam of anticipation deepened the hue of her cobalt eyes. "Next April. That'll give us a year to plan."

"And a year for Bonnie and Scott to make sure this union is God's will," Dad added.

"Oh, Daddy. We *are* sure."

Bill Stenson sent his youngest daughter a look saying the topic wasn't open for discussion. Mel knew that expression well.

Does Dad have his doubts?

"Bonnie, next April will come soon enough. The months will zoom right by. You'll see."

"Your mom's right," Scott said, stretching an arm around Bonnie's slender shoulders.

Watching the scene, Melody felt a headache coming on. "I think I'll turn in." She massaged her right temple where it had begun to throb.

"Yeah, I'd best get home, too," Luke said. "Nice meeting you." He sent a single nod in Scott's direction before smiling a good-bye at all three of the Stensons. "Great to see you folks again."

"I'll walk you out, Luke." Mel turned. "Night, everyone."

Amidst the calls of farewells and "sweet dreams," Melody distinctly heard Scott say, "G'night, Mellow."

She missed a step and suddenly felt as though she might be physically ill.

Mellow! Scott called her *Mellow!*

Dazed, she trailed Luke through the kitchen and out into the dimly lit back hall where the handle on her tightly reined emotions slipped.

"Luke," she whispered, grabbing the front of his shirt, "did you hear what he just called me? Did you hear that?"

"Melody—" There was a note of alarm in his voice as he caught her wrists.

"He called me 'Mellow.' How dare he! That's what he used to call me when—when we. . ."

The words jammed in her throat and tears clouded her vision. She yanked her hands free from Luke's grasp and buried her face in them.

Then the sobs started.

❧

Luke stood by, feeling as helpless as a boy while Melody cried her eyes out. He fought the urge to march back into the dining room and sock Ramsay a good one for hurting Melody like he had.

"Shh. Don't cry," he whispered.

She sagged against him, and Luke enfolded her in most proper embrace he could manage.

Oh, Lord, please don't let Bill Stenson find us here in the back hall like this. I'll have a lot of explaining to do.

A heartbeat later, Luke shook off his trepidation. Melody was hurting. She needed a hug. She needed a hero—and here was just one more chance where Luke could fulfill that coveted role.

"Shh, Melody, don't cry," he said again, resting his cheek on the top of her head. Strands of her short hair tickled his lips.

He tightened his hold on her, and the realization hit: After spending the day with her, Melody Cartwright was in his arms! A dream come true—well, sort of. He would have preferred she wasn't spilling tears all over him because of another guy.

"I really l–loved him." Melody sniffed. "I was so s–stupid."

"We've all done stupid things." Luke grimaced; he hadn't meant to agree. "I mean, we all make mistakes, and it's the lesson God taught you that's important."

He felt her nod, heard another sloppy sniff, and with one hand, reached into the back pocket of his jeans, hoping he still had a tissue or two. He sighed with relief when he found a couple still folded there.

"Here." Luke set them into Melody's palm.

She moved backward and dabbed her eyes, then blew her nose.

"Sorry, Luke. That was rude of me."

"Thar she blows," he teased.

Melody smiled, and Luke felt like his mission had been accomplished. But seconds later, her sadness returned. She sniffed again.

"How am I going to survive this next year?" Her voice was barely audible. "Scott will be here all the time, as a constant reminder of my stupid naïveté. This is so humiliating."

"I'll help you through it, Melody—me and all your other friends. And you've got the most important Friend of all on your side: Jesus Christ."

She didn't reply.

"It might sound trite because you're hurting right now, but Jesus really is the One you've got to hang on to through all this."

"You're right. Thanks, Luke." She leaned against him again, this time in an awkward show of gratitude.

"Better now?"

"Yeah. Better. Thanks."

"Anytime."

With that, Luke leaned forward and placed a kiss on Melody's cheek. He took his time about it, relishing the feel of his lips against her petal-soft skin. He wished he could kiss away all the angst she felt inside. But that privilege didn't belong to him—not yet anyway.

As he wished her a good night and walked around the yard to his place, Luke felt more determined than ever to win Melody's heart.

six

On Sunday morning Melody sat between her friends Sarah Canterfield and Jamie Becker while on the other side of the sanctuary, a small crowd had gathered around the Stensons. Eager friends stood in line to meet Scott.

Sarah gawked. "Is that Bonnie's fiancé?"

"Where?" Jamie, sitting on Mel's right, squinted her eyes. "Oh, there. Yeah, he's gorgeous, huh? I met him during Bible study this morning."

Melody's heart sank. It seemed nobody saw through to the real Scott. But she felt forced to go along with crowd. "He's okay."

"Just 'okay'?" Jamie nudged her as if you say, *Are you blind?*

"Well, you know what I mean." Turning, she noticed her friend's brown eyes sparked with curiosity. "Beauty, or in this case handsomeness, is in the eye of the beholder."

"Whatever." Jamie folded her long, skinny arms. "I think Bonnie ordered that guy off the cover of a macho-man magazine."

Mel flung a gaze toward the arched ceiling.

"Aren't you happy for Bonnie?" Sarah asked. "She's your sister."

"Of course I'm happy." Melody's conscience wouldn't allow her to finish the sentence. Happy? No, her heart ached, and she feared for her younger sister's future with a man like Scott Ramsay. She opened her Bible and stared at it, unseeing.

"Oh, I get it." Jamie's naturally deep voice was now laden with sarcasm. "You're jealous, and your apathy is just a cover."

Mel clapped her Bible shut. "I'm hardly apathetic." She was

surprised by her own harsh tone.

Her friends exchanged curious glances, and Mel regretted getting drawn in to this juvenile banter.

Melody reopened her Bible and leafed through its delicate pages. She considered her two friends, whom she'd known for years. She'd heard people say Jamie wasn't pretty, that she was too skinny and plain. The words were unkind, however true, but Jamie's outward appearance didn't bother Melody. She tried to see the best in people—see their inner beauty. After all, she'd learned the hard way with Scott that a handsome face often didn't reach beyond the cheekbones. But now with Jamie, Mel saw it wasn't anything physical that caused her friend to seem unattractive; it was Jamie's cynicism.

"I feel a lot of things about Bonnie's engagement," Mel said, trying to explain herself in lieu of Jamie's "apathetic" remark. She felt the need to make peace with her terse emotions before the service began, and she promised herself she'd sort out all her feelings later, once she was alone.

"Are you just a little jealous of Bonnie?" Sarah asked. "I mean, it wouldn't be normal if you weren't. I'd be green with envy if my younger sister snagged the handsome prince and left me looking like the old maid."

"Old maid? Thanks a lot."

"Oh, you know what I mean." Sarah laughed and tucked strands of her sienna-colored hair behind one ear. The silver earrings she wore swung from her lobes.

"So are you jealous or not?" Jamie persisted.

"No, I am *not* jealous." Mel felt she spoke the truth, too. Sure, she'd felt the pangs of envy when she first learned that Bonnie would be getting married, but had her sister become engaged to any other guy, that initial resentment would have worn off by now.

What Melody felt inside were feelings she didn't want to describe—and they were all directed at Scott. That man had stolen her heart, stomped all over it, and he wasn't even sorry! Worse, he was now engaged to her little sister.

"I think you're jealous," Sarah said in a singsong voice. She leaned into Mel and something between amusement and intrigue glimmered in her emerald-colored eyes.

"Thanks for giving me the benefit of the doubt, *girlfriend*." Melody collected her purse and Bible, stood, and stepped over Sarah's white stocking-clad legs. "Now I know how Job felt."

"Oh, get a grip," came Jamie's insensitive reply.

Melody ignored it and strode down the side aisle just as the lights dimmed and the choir began to sing. She spoke to no one as she walked through the foyer and exited the front doors.

The April sunshine peeked through fluffy clouds and warmed Mel's face and arms. She had every intention of hopping in her car and driving off to Anywhere, USA. Her fight-or-flight responses had kicked in and flight won out; however, she suddenly remembered her car was at home. Dad had taken one look at it this morning and decided it would have to be towed to the mechanic's tomorrow. So Melody rode to church with her parents.

An expletive made it as far as Melody's lips before she choked it back down. Where had that awful word come from? She didn't talk like that. And why did she feel so hateful and angry?

There in the parking lot, she lowered her head. *Lord, forgive me. I'm a mess. Why is this happening?*

She gazed at the blue sky above, and her heart seemed to say she needed to hear Pastor's message. She spun around and walked back into the church building.

The lobby was now bustling as choir members made their way from the front to their seats. Mel wrapped her arms around her Bible, holding it close, and just stared through the narrow windows of the sanctuary's doors. She wasn't sure if she should go in and find a place to sit or stay in the foyer for the service.

❧

Luke sang with the choir as he did every Sunday morning. As he was making his way through the lobby, he spotted Melody across the way. She wore one of those wrinkly skirts, the kind his sister said were twisted around a broomstick or some such thing. It was beige with a navy print and with it she wore a silky, dark blue blouse. A crinkly shawl that matched her skirt was slung over her shoulders.

Luke's appreciative gaze moved upward still until it rested on Melody's face. Judging by her forlorn expression, she felt miserable. Luke stepped forward and before he really had the chance to think things through, he found himself at her side.

"Good morning." He tried to sound his cheery best.

She gave him quick glance. "Oh, hi, Luke."

"Are you going in?" He nodded toward the sanctuary.

"I'm thinking about it. I—I just don't know."

Luke guessed she didn't want to sit with her family because of Ramsay.

Melody turned and faced him. Her indigo eyes were filled with unshed tears. "You know what? You're the only one who understands what I'm going through. My friends don't understand, and my family won't either."

Luke wasn't about to debate the latter, although he knew the Stensons were reasonable people. But his heart ached for Melody. "Want to sit with me?"

She replied with an almost indiscernible little nod.

He placed his hand at the small of her back and led her to the main doors of the sanctuary, then down the middle aisle where he found two seats on the right-hand side. He allowed Melody to slip into the row of cushioned seats first before claiming the chair on the end. The congregation had just finished singing the classic hymn "Make Me a Channel of Blessing."

Melody leaned into him. "Thanks, Luke. You've been a blessing to me." Her voice was but a whisper.

"Anytime." Luke's spirit soared.

❧

Melody spent Sunday afternoon holed up in her bedroom. Bonnie and Scott went to lunch with a half dozen of Bonnie's friends. Melody and Luke had been invited, but he had a house showing this afternoon and Melody refused to be in Scott Ramsay's company any longer than necessary. So she rode home with her parents and now, while Mom and Dad tinkered around downstairs, Mel checked her e-mail and worked on her online assignments for the college courses in which she'd enrolled. She tried to keep her mind busy but those haunting thoughts seemed to prevail.

Bonnie's getting married—I should be the one getting married. I'm the oldest!

She chose my colors for her wedding—my colors!

My dream is becoming Bonnie's reality—it's totally not fair!

Mel powered down her computer and decided to read. She went downstairs and pulled out sections from the Sunday newspaper and retreated back upstairs to her side of the room. Sitting cross-legged on her bed, she poured over the news, hoping to find an article about someone whose life's crisis was a whole lot worse than hers.

To her shame, she found several.

Around suppertime, Bonnie and Mom entered the room. Bonnie carried a pizza box.

"I bought dinner," she announced.

"I have the cola," Mom mimicked.

Mel looked up from the newspaper.

"We decided it's girl-talk time," Mom said, positioning herself on the end of Melody's bed.

"Sure." Girl-talk time was a habitual thing around here. She always figured their discussions kept them a close family.

Collecting the newspaper, Mel tossed it on the floor beside her bed. She felt starved. She hadn't eaten much lunch.

"Thanks, Bon-bon. This smells delicious!"

"It's your favorite," Bonnie said as she handed out thick napkins.

The cynical side of Melody emerged. "My favorite pizza? What's the catch?"

Mom laughed and took a slice of the stuffed-crust, garden veggie delight. "You'll see."

"Well," her sister began, picking off all the black olives on her piece of pizza, "I want you to be my maid of honor, so I thought I'd bribe you with food."

Mel was touched. "You don't have to bribe me. Of course I'll be your maid of honor!"

"*Now* you tell me," Bonnie quipped, "after I spent fourteen bucks on this pizza."

All three women shared a laugh.

They ate and Bonnie talked about her lineup. Mel, as maid of honor, Susan, their cousin, would be a bridesmaid along with their friends Terri, Sonya, Amy, and Debbie.

Those would have been my choices. Mel set down her second slice of pizza. Suddenly she'd lost her appetite.

Her mother seemed to sense Mel's mood change. "There is something else we need to discuss."

"What's that?" Mel glanced at the now somber expressions on her mother's and Bonnie's faces.

"It's Scott," Bonnie blurted. "He told me that the two of you dated in Madison."

"He told you that?" Mel felt wary. She would have liked to hear Scott's version of "dating." Mel had little doubt his terminology differed vastly from hers.

"Of course. Scott and I have no secrets between us."

Whatever, Mel thought, her heart like a stone.

"Scott said you mistook the casual dating, you know, two

friends going out for a hamburger, as something more serious," Bonnie relayed. "He feels like you hate him now."

"I do hate him." Mel caught herself. "Well, I mean—hatred is a sin, I know that. But I—um—dislike Scott greatly. How's that?"

"That's not acceptable," Mom said. "Scott is going to be part of this family, and you need to love him, first as a brother in Christ and next as your brother-in-law."

"I'm working on it," Mel replied, picking at her pizza. "It's just that—it was just a shock to see him yesterday."

"Why didn't you tell your father and me about Scott if you were dating him?" A stern, parental spark entered Mom's blue eyes. "And if you felt serious about him?"

"I had planned to bring Scott home over spring break, but he'd disappeared by then." Melody looked at Bonnie. "Did he tell you that he just up and took off, leaving a lot of broken hearts behind?"

"Scott ran out of money," Bonnie explained. "The university forced him to drop out. He moved back to Iowa and lived with his dad for a while before returning to Wisconsin. He finished his bachelors at UW-Oshkosh. He graduated with honors." Bonnie beamed. "Now he lives in one of the apartment buildings his mom owns. He manages the building for her as well as working at the hospital."

Melody bit back a retort.

"Scott's parents are divorced," Mom said.

"Yeah, I seem to recall that was the case."

"He feels bad that you took your relationship with him more seriously than he ever did," Bonnie said.

"Oh, how considerate of him to feel bad," Mel all but spat before the whole, ugly truth poured out. "For your information, our relationship was more than just 'two friends going out for a hamburger.' Scott said he loved me, Bonnie. He said he wanted to spend the rest of his life with me." Mel ignored the way her sister seemed to pale. "I was naïve, I'll admit it. I believed every word he said. What's more. . ." Melody gulped down her shame. "I allowed Scott some privileges that I shouldn't have."

"Like what?" Mom appeared appalled—and Mel figured she had the right to be.

"Like kissing, inappropriate touching." Melody felt her face flame with disgrace. "I've asked for God's forgiveness. It wasn't right. You brought me up better than that." She looked back at her mother. "I was just so in love with Scott. He knew it and took advantage of me."

"Did you—and Scott. . ." Bonnie looked like she might cry. "Did you?"

Melody instinctively knew what her sister wanted to know. "No, we didn't go that far."

Relief flooded Bonnie's features, and her slender shoulders sagged.

"Why didn't you say something when you came home from college, Mel?"

She turned her gaze on Mom again. "I was embarrassed, and I knew I'd done wrong." Mel drew in a deep breath. "There were other women, too." She looked at Bonnie. "He didn't just tell me he loved me. He told lots of girls he loved them. We all found each other after Scott disappeared because. . . Well, we were all searching for him. We were worried about him, initially. After that, we all wanted to lynch him."

"I—I need to check this out." Bonnie rose from the side of the bed, grabbed her cell phone from off her desk, and strode out to the back porch.

Melody felt somewhat insulted that Bonnie hadn't taken her word for it.

"You wouldn't make this up, Mel, would you?"

Mel's eyes widened at the implication. "Mom, how can you ask me that? I'm not a liar."

"But if you're hurt, you might want to drive a wedge between Bonnie and Scott."

"No, but, I'd like to drive a wedge through Scott's heart— make that a stake."

"Melody, how can you spout such evil?"

A grin slipped out. "Well, I was mostly joking."

"It wasn't funny."

All mirth disappeared. "But that's how I feel." She closed her eyes, despising the hatefulness inside of her. "Mom, I'm still hurt. Yes, that part is true. But I'd never be manipulative and lie—and I'd never want to hurt Bonnie."

Mom seemed satisfied with the answer and finished her piece of pizza.

Minutes later, Bonnie reentered the bedroom, closing the patio door with a decisive slam. "Scott said what you told us is pure fabrication."

"What?" Mel brought her chin back in surprise. She expected Scott to deny it, but she didn't think Bonnie would take his word over hers.

"You're lying, Melody, because you want to break up Scott and me."

"I have no intentions of coming between you and Scott." Mel stood. "And I'm not the liar, Bonnie, he is. I can give you names, and you can personally ask the women he hurt. One even carried Scott's child, and she had an abortion!"

A gasp emanated from Mom's lips.

"No! That's not true." Bonnie's face turned an angry shade of scarlet. "Scott said he dated you and maybe one other girl from SFC. He said he always made it clear you were just friends because he knew he had to go on to med school."

"He's a liar, Bonnie." Mel held her ground.

"No, he's not!"

Mom stood. "All right. That's enough. I don't know how we'll resolve this, but for now, this discussion is over."

Bonnie stomped toward the bedroom's entryway. "I'm retracting my offer," she told Melody, her hand on the doorknob. "I don't want you to be my maid of honor."

Mel suddenly felt as though she'd had a stake driven through *her* heart. She glanced at her mother. "You believe me, don't you?"

"I want to be fair to the both of you." She pushed her blond hair from her forehead. "I don't know what to believe anymore."

"You think I'm lying?" Tears gathered in Melody's eyes and her throat constricted. She felt accused—convicted without a fair trial.

"Like I said, this discussion is over until I speak with your father."

With that, Mom left the room, and Mel felt like her heart had been smashed to bits.

For a second time.

seven

Luke parked his SUV then killed the engine. Leaning toward the passenger seat, he grabbed his suit coat, along with the bag containing the foot-long submarine sandwich he purchased on his way home. He climbed out of his vehicle, locked it, and headed for the house. After this afternoon's showing, he'd gone back to church for the evening service. He didn't see Melody there, but hadn't expected to; the Stensons weren't a family that habitually attended church on Sunday nights.

Darkness had descended and the neighborhood was quiet as Luke ambled up the narrow sidewalk toward his two-story home. He glanced up at Melody's bedroom window. The light was on, but the back porch door closed. Sometimes when the evening air was mild, like tonight, Luke caught glimpses of Melody sitting on the adjoining porch. He always called a "hello" and she replied in a neighborly way, but the exchange never developed into conversation, much to Luke's disappointment. However, after yesterday and this morning, he felt hopeful—hopeful, but cautious. He didn't want to make a pest of himself, and he couldn't shake the gnawing fear that one of these times when he approached her, Melody would flat out refuse him.

Luke reached his side door and flipped through his key ring for his house key. It was at that moment he heard something. Something odd. A cat? No. He listened then decided what he heard were guttural, unadulterated sobs.

He frowned. Melody?

Pivoting, he glanced up at her bedroom window again then decided the sound was much closer. Had he missed her sitting on the upper porch?

Luke stepped back a few paces, but couldn't see anyone on the small wooden balcony. His gaze traveled downward and across the Stensons' backyard.

He finally spotted her. She sat on the ground, just behind the tree, her back against the garage, and she was most definitely crying.

Helplessness enveloped him. What should he do? Go over and try to comfort her? What if she told him to mind his own business?

Luke had an older sister, so he was familiar with those female hysteria jags. Sometimes they were a result of the most illogical circumstances; however, in this case, Luke knew Melody was struggling with her feelings for Scott Ramsay. And Luke would like nothing better than to rid her thoughts of that guy.

But if I go over there, will I be her hero or her number one nuisance?

A few more seconds passed, and Luke decided to brave it. It pained him to hear Melody cry.

Leaving his suit coat and bagged sandwich in between the doors, he traipsed down the walkway, praying for the words to comfort Melody—and praying she'd allow him to comfort her. As he walked up her yard's sidewalk, Luke prayed for calm.

He reached Melody and slowly hunkered down beside her. She hadn't noticed him yet. He touched her shoulder, knowing he'd likely startle her one way or another.

He did.

She jumped. "Luke! You scared me half to death!"

"I'm sorry. Are you okay? I—I saw you from my yard."

She didn't reply right away, but choked out another sob. "No, I'm not okay," she stated at last. "M—my whole family hates me. I t—told my mom and B—Bonnie about dating Scott. I told them the whole truth, but S—Scott denied it. They believe him over m—me! Then Mom told Dad, and now my d–dad's angry with me because three years ago when I dated S–Scott. . ." Melody sniffed and gulped, and Luke began searching his pockets for a tissue. "I should have called and asked his permission. My dad says he's so disappointed in me, and Bonnie said I can't be her maid of honor."

Her arms wrapped around her knees, Melody lowered her head and let out another round of gut-wrenching sobs.

"Shh, Melody." He rubbed his palm across her shoulder blades. That powerless feeling crept over him again. "Oh, no. I don't even have any tissues."

He'd muttered the latter, not really intending for her to hear, but she did. In reply, she held up the tissue box hiding under her denim-clad legs.

"This was a planned sob session," she informed him with a hiccup.

That she was weeping at all moved Luke to compassion. "Aw, Mellie." Speechless, he just continued to give her a back rub.

"You know, I don't think anyone has called me 'Mellie' since I was in grade school."

"Did that bother you? I'm sorry."

"No, it didn't bother me." Beneath the little bit of glow radiating from a neighboring yard light, Luke saw a little smile break through her tear-streaked face.

"Want some company, or should I leave you alone?"

Melody regarded him while resting the side of her head on her knee. "I don't know."

"Here. Scoot over."

She complied and Luke positioned himself beside her. He soon realized they sat on the slab that usually supported the Stensons' tall, plastic garbage bins. Since tomorrow was trash day, he assumed the bins were in the alley. He'd been so preoccupied that he had likely strolled right past them.

He also discovered there wasn't a lot of room on this cement platform. He and Melody sat hip to hip.

For several long minutes neither spoke. Luke wished he knew just the right thing to say, but, at the present, words failed him.

Melody dabbed her eyes and blew her nose. She seemed to have calmed down.

"You smell nice, Luke."

"What?" He wasn't sure he'd heard her correctly.

"Your cologne or aftershave—whatever it is—it smells good."

"Thanks." He felt embarrassment warm his face. "I'm surprised you can even smell after your—um—*sob session*."

He heard her soft laugh as she leaned her arms on her knees, then placed her head on her arms.

Several more moments went by.

"You know? You showed up just when I needed you," Melody said in a broken little voice. "I was thinking about packing up my stuff and taking off in my car. But then I remembered my car's not drivable."

Luke sensed more tears were on the way. He put his arm around her. "Don't cry anymore, Melody, all right?"

She moved her head to his shoulder, and Luke suddenly felt like the luckiest guy in the world. For the second time in twenty-four hours he held the girl of his dreams in his arms.

Then, much to his utter chagrin, his stomach moaned in hunger.

"Was that you?"

"Um—yeah. I didn't get any supper tonight."

"You're hungry!"

"Obviously." He laughed and thought of his foot-long sub. "Hey, want to split my sandwich with me? I bought it at a sub shop on the way home. Nice and fresh. . ."

Melody sat up on her haunches. "Can I cook something for you instead? I love to cook, and it'll get my mind off my troubles."

"Are you kidding? You can cook for me anytime you

want." A vision of Melody moving about his kitchen amidst mouthwatering aromas flitted through Luke's mind. It was a notion he never dared to entertain. Could this really be a dream come true? "I—um—don't cook much."

"I don't know many single guys who do." She stood.

Luke did the same and took a mental inventory of his cupboards and refrigerator. He tamped down his sudden disappointment. "There's just one problem."

"And that is?"

"I don't think I have any food in the house to cook."

Melody actually giggled. "Luke, you *bachelor*."

"Is that a dirty word?" He grinned.

"In our career group it is."

Luke chuckled. He knew Mel referred to the overabundance of single women who joined the career group at church in order to snag a spouse. Sometimes they were successful, other times they weren't. But he never sensed Melody was husband hunting. Of course, if she'd been harboring feelings for Ramsay that could explain it.

"Well, what about tomorrow night?" Melody asked, drawing Luke from his thoughts. "Can I cook for you then? You've been so sweet this weekend, and I'd like a chance to repay you for all your kindness." She sniffed again then bent to fetch the tissue box which she tucked under one arm. "You said you wanted to be there for me, and you have been."

"Tomorrow's fine." Could this be happening? Luke wanted to pinch himself to make sure he wasn't hallucinating.

"I get off at four thirty, and I'll stop at the store. . . ." Melody paused in midsentence. "Oh, Luke, I forgot! I'll be without wheels for a while. My dad's having my car towed to his mechanic in the morning."

"I'll pick you up, and we can stop at the store afterward." The offer flew out of Luke's mouth before he had a chance consider it. Well, he could adjust his schedule.

"Really? You'll pick me up from work?"

"Sure. Want me to drive you there in the morning, too?" Luke felt close to giddy. He took Melody's hand and bowed over it. "Your wish is my command, milady."

To his dismay his antics were rewarded with more tears.

Placing his hands on Melody's shoulders, he leaned slightly forward, trying to glimpse her face. "What's wrong? I was kidding around."

"You're so n—nice and I don't deserve it. I feel s—so hateful."

"Will you stop it?"

The next moment, she was in his arms again, and Luke thought he could get used to holding her this way. A heartbeat later, he chastened himself for such thoughts. This woman was distraught and here he was thinking of his own selfish desires.

"Mellie, don't cry." He stroked the back of her hair, marveling how thick and soft it felt against his fingers. "Give yourself a break. You're going through a tough time."

She didn't reply, and Luke didn't move—until a disconcerting thought whirled through his brain.

"Say, Melody? If your dad comes out. . . I mean, I wouldn't want him to catch us like this. It might not look so great, especially since he's already unhappy about—"

Before he could finish, she took a quick step backward.

"You're absolutely right. I didn't think—it was so innocent, you know?"

"I know."

Luke felt a twinge of regret in voicing his concern since it meant loosing his hold on Melody. However, not thirty seconds later, the bright yard light went on, and Bill Stenson's voice boomed through the backyard.

"Melody? Mel, where you?"

"I'm here, Dad."

He appeared on the walk and squinted in their direction.

"How long does it take to roll the garbage carts into the alley?"

"I'm—talking with Luke." She turned and gave Luke a grateful stare.

He let out a breath of relief and sent up a prayer of thanks. He would have hated to get Melody in worse trouble with her folks. What's more, Bill Stenson's trust was important to Luke. He'd hate to do something foolish and lose it forever.

"Well, hurry it up, will you?" Bill said, sounding gruff. "I want to lock up for the night. If I have to get you to work by eight and then—"

"Luke says he'll drive me."

A pause. "Naw, we're not bothering the neighbors."

"No bother, Mr. Stenson," Luke put in. "I offered."

The older man stood, arms akimbo while mulling it over. "Okay, fine. That'll work. Thanks."

"My pleasure."

Mr. Stenson strode back into the house.

Melody looked up at Luke and gave him a tenuous smile. Under the beaming yard light, he could see the sadness in her eyes and her tearstained face. He wished he could kiss away all her sorrow.

"My dad's angry with me."

"He'll get over it. He loves you. Besides, you told the truth, something you had to do even though it was difficult. That took courage."

In spite of her nod, Melody's bottom lip quivered. She lowered her chin and gazed at the white leather athletic shoes she wore on her feet.

"So what time do you want to leave in the morning?"

She looked back up at him. "Is seven thirty all right?"

Luke nodded. "I'll pull out front."

"Thanks."

He tipped his head, considering her circumspectly. "Are you still going to cook for me tomorrow night?"

"You bet." She sent him a determined grin before turning around and jogging toward the house.

❧

Melody saw Luke's Durango from the living room window. She snatched her purse off the coffee table and headed for the front door.

"I'm leaving," she called before slamming the door on any reply.

She bristled as she walked to the waiting SUV. No one was talking to anyone else unless it proved absolutely necessary, although Bonnie wasn't speaking to Melody at all.

She opened the door and climbed up into the passenger seat.

"Good morning." Luke sent her a sunny smile, a stark contrast to the gloomy skies overhead.

"Are you always this happy?" Mel teased, strapping on her seat belt.

"Only when I'm in good company." Luke headed the SUV down the street.

"Well, you can't be referring to me. I'm so angry. Scott Ramsay is tearing my family apart." She grit her teeth before adding, "I've just got to do something about it—about him."

"You know, Melody, I've been thinking and praying about this situation, and I'm wondering if—well, the anger you feel. . ." Luke stopped for a red light and looked over at her. "Do you think you're still in love with Scott?"

"No. I hashed this all out in my head last night. I've concluded that if Scott would have apologized to me instead of pretending he didn't remember me I probably could forgive him. It's just that seeing him again made all that old hurt come back, and then he added insult to injury."

"I understand." The light changed and Luke accelerated through the intersection. "So it's a forgiveness issue then?"

"Yeah, I guess it is," Melody admitted. "And I know what I

have to do—in fact, I've done it. I couldn't sleep all night, so very early this morning I knelt beside my bed and poured my heart out to God." Tears welled in her eyes, but Mel blinked them back. "I asked Him to help me forgive Scott, but I have to tell you, Luke, revenge is so much more appealing."

He laughed and pulled into the trendy coffee shop's parking lot. "We've got a few minutes, and I need some coffee. Want a cup?"

"Sure." Melody smiled.

"Cream? Sugar?"

"Heavy on both."

"Got it."

Luke hopped out of the SUV and disappeared into the building. Watching him go, Mel decided he sure was a special guy—a special friend. She wondered again who he was "crazy" about. If Luke displayed as much caring and kindness to that woman as he had to Mel this last weekend, then Mystery Girl would definitely be aware that he cared.

She'd probably even fall in love with him.

eight

Dinner will be ready in about an hour and a half." Mel stood over Luke's stove, browning the ground beef in preparation for making her famous belly-busting lasagna. At first, she had considered grilling outdoors since the spring weather had been unseasonably warm for April. But the morning clouds never departed, and this afternoon, the wind shifted. The temperature plummeted. Local weather channels reported a thunderstorm was on its way, so Mel decided to create her specialty for Luke. "I hope seven o'clock isn't too late for you to eat."

"Seven is perfect," Luke replied. He stood several feet away, leaning against the wall with his arms folded, watching her cook. "I had a late lunch today."

Melody peered over her shoulder at him. He still wore his navy suit and lavender shirt, minus the jacket and tie. "I hope you'll like my lasagna. My family nags me to make it for them all the time."

"I'm sure I'll enjoy it. I love Italian food."

"Just to forewarn you, I don't know how authentic my version is." She grinned. "I sort of improvised on a recipe I found in a magazine and it turned out really well. I've been making lasagna this way ever since." She glanced at him again then moved to the chopping block where she diced an onion. "Was your mom a good cook?"

Luke shrugged and unfurled his arms before sauntering over to the kitchen table. Pulling out one of the Windsor chairs, he sat down. "Mom didn't cook a whole lot, but when she did meals were always tasty, as I recall."

"Why didn't she cook much? Didn't she enjoy it?"

"Oh, I don't know if it was so much that. Mom was just always preoccupied with whatever article she was writing. But as kids, we thought potpies and TV dinners were great."

Mel's smile grew as she imagined the Berringers' family life. Luke's dad had been a truck driver and his mother worked for the *Milwaukee Sentinel*, a daily morning newspaper that had since merged with the *Milwaukee Journal*. She remembered Luke's folks as kindhearted, churchgoing people.

But the house, itself, looked quite different than what she recalled. Melody had been inside this place a number of times, since she and Luke's sister, Amber, had occasionally played together in spite of their age difference. And if Mel's memory served her correctly, this kitchen was once paneled in a red brick and had a coppery-colored linoleum on the floor. Now, however, everything was white from the walls to the window blinds, countertops, cupboards, appliances, and ceramic flooring. Much too sterile for Mel's tastes, but it would be fun to decorate it and give it some color.

"When did you remodel the kitchen?"

"After my folks died. I sort of went into a remodeling mode, thinking Amber and I would sell the house. But then I liked the changes. It felt like it was a whole different place when I finished, so I bought out Amber's half and decided to stay."

"I'm glad you did." She gave him a smile before turning to deposit the onions into the browning meat. "But don't you ever feel lonely, living here all by yourself?"

"Sometimes, but I keep busy."

Melody returned back to the chopping block where a plump green pepper awaited its turn under the knife. She grinned at Luke. "You could ask your mystery girl over for dinner one night. I'll even cook for the two of you."

He laughed. "I knew something like that was coming." He chuckled again. "I think I'll let God take care of my 'mystery girl,' all right?"

"All right. I'll mind my own business." Mel started to slice the pepper.

Their conversation lagged.

"Listen, Melody, I appreciate your offer. I really do."

"Oh, I'm not insulted or anything. I was just trying to help."

"I know, and I appreciate it."

"And you're right about leaving the matter in God's hands. I wish I would have done that with Scott. I was so crazy about him that I practically threw myself at the man." She arched a brow. "Of course, he didn't seem to mind at the time."

She chopped up the green pepper with more force than necessary before scraping the tiny pieces into the meat mixture. Next, she prepared a white sauce, which she used instead of ricotta cheese.

"I've been looking forward to your cooking all day."

Melody smiled, feeling pleased by his remark and the change of subject.

With the meat browned and the added vegetables sautéed, she preheated the oven. Lifting the jar of sauce, she tried to open its lid, but the thing wouldn't budge.

She handed the jar to Luke who twisted the cap off with little effort.

"Show-off."

He chuckled and Mel reclaimed the jar.

"Now, if I were a *real* chef," she told him, "I'd make my sauce from scratch. But this stuff's pretty good."

She poured the tomato sauce over the meat and then stirred it. In the meantime, the water for her noodles had come to a boil. After parboiling the pasta, she placed the first layer in the bottom of a greased rectangular ceramic baking dish.

Layer by layer, Mel assembled her creation. Noodles, meat sauce, white sauce, mozzarella cheese. Noodles, meat sauce, white sauce, mozzarella cheese. When she'd filled the entire pan, Mel topped it off with a generous sprinkling of Parmesan cheese.

"Okay, now lift this baby, Luke." She laughed.

He stood, crossed the room, and did as she bid him. "Whoa, that's one serious lasagna!"

"Want to put it in the oven for me—since you're such a *he-man?*"

Luke replied with a smirk, but slid the pan in the oven. Then he rubbed his palms together. "Let's catch the news while dinner's cooking."

"Okay, sure."

Melody followed him into the living room. Luke sat on the leather couch, and she situated herself in one of the matching armchairs. Remote in hand, Luke flipped on his wide-screen TV and tuned in to one of the cable news channels known for its conservative views. Meanwhile, thunder rumbled in the distance.

"I hope we have a good thunderstorm tonight."

Luke regarded her with a grin. "You like storms?"

She nodded. "I especially like to curl up on the couch with a quilt and read a good mystery. But if it's too suspenseful, I get freaked out and turn on every light on in the house which causes my dad to have a fit because he pays the electric bill."

Luke chuckled.

"Do you read a lot?"

"Not as much as I used to."

"As I recall, you were sort of a bookworm." She laughed as another memory surfaced. "Hey, do you remember how you got into trouble for spying on Bonnie and me through our bedroom window with that telescope of yours?"

Luke's guffaw filled the room. "I can't believe you still remember that!"

"I do—and, whew! Your dad was really mad."

"I was probably acting out the latest adventure novel I'd read. But I never saw anything scandalous, you have my word."

"Back then there wasn't much to see, Luke," she teased.

"Regardless, I got a lickin' and I deserved it. You can't let little boys turn into peeping toms."

Melody laughed. So, Luke had been a typical little boy after all. It had always seemed to her that he was teacher's perfect pet. It used to annoy Mel to no end.

The hour flew by and when the lasagna finished cooking, Mel removed it from the oven. While it cooled, she threw together a salad, and Luke set the dining room table.

Then, just as she and Luke were about to dish up their meal, Bonnie and Scott showed up at the side door.

"Dad sent us over to tell you there's a severe thunderstorm warning," Bonnie said after Luke asked the couple in. "He'd like you home before it hits."

Melody heard the terseness in her sister's voice and wondered if their dad sent Bonnie over to try to coax along the reconciliation process. "I'll be home soon. Luke and I are just about to eat."

Scott spotted the pan of lasagna. "Wow, that looks terrific and I'm starved."

"We just had dinner." Bonnie gave him a frown.

"I know, but all those vegetables you served—they were good and everything, except they don't stick with a guy very long."

He winked at Melody and she turned away, unimpressed by his attempted charm. She busied herself by carrying the salad plates into the dining room, praying Luke wouldn't invite Bonnie and Scott to share their supper.

"So is this like a romantic dinner for two or something?" Scott asked when Mel returned to the kitchen.

"You've got half of it right," Mel quipped. "It's for *two*."

Luke wiped his palm across his mouth in an obvious effort to hide his smirk.

"I don't think I've seen lasagna ever look that good."

What a beggar, Mel thought.

Bonnie hooked her arm around Scott's. "Let's go home, and

I'll make you something to eat there."

"But they've got plenty here," he argued. Dressed in a plaid shirt that hung over his baggy blue jeans, he not only looked like a seventeen-year-old punk, but Mel thought he behaved like one, too. "That pan would feed eight people."

He turned to Luke. "Come on, buddy, what do you say? Can Bonnie and I join you two?"

Luke flicked his brown-eyed gaze in Mel's direction, and she could almost *feel* the battle warring within him. Scott had put Luke's back to the wall, and Luke was far too polite to tell Scott to buzz off. Melody, on the other hand, might have the nerve to say it, but this wasn't her house.

She turned and pulled two more plates from the cupboard. Again, Luke glanced her way. She gave him a single nod then walked into the dining room, where she heard Luke say, "Sure. You two are welcome to stay for dinner."

❧

Two days later, on Wednesday afternoon, Luke stared out his kitchen window. Melody had just pulled up and parked in the carport. He felt a tad disappointed that her vehicle was now repaired. He'd enjoyed driving Melody to and from work the last couple of days.

But now she didn't need him anymore—at least not as her chauffeur.

He wished and prayed that he could still be her hero if things remained difficult between Melody and her family. From what she told him this morning, tensions still ran high in the Stenson home—even after Monday night's dinner. Luke had hoped sharing a meal would help patch things up between the sisters, but the unpleasant nuance at the table that night was unmistakable. Bonnie's anger and resentment. . . Melody's deep sense of hurt and betrayal. . . The only one who'd enjoyed himself was Scott.

Afterward, Luke privately apologized for caving in to Ramsay's request. But Melody understood his predicament. In the days following, Luke must have told her a dozen times that she could cook for him whenever she needed a stress reliever, and Melody said she'd take him up on the offer.

But would she really?

She needs a reason to spend time with me. I need time to win her heart.

Luke watched as Melody, attired in the light blue scrubs and white T-shirt she wore to work, ambled up the walkway to her house. Her dad had fetched her this afternoon then drove her to the mechanic's shop. Luke thought the guy had worked fast, but apparently he'd just fixed Melody's car so it was drivable until all the parts for the bodywork arrived.

A pity, Luke mused. He would have liked to continue driving Melody to work and back, especially since she'd decided to forgo the expense of a rental.

At that moment, Bill Stenson's blue truck proceeded up the alley and turned into the garage. It'd be just like Mr. Stenson to follow his daughter home to ensure she arrived safely, seeing as how she'd just had her car fixed.

Luke moved away from the window and made his way through the dining room, living room, then rounded the corner and climbed the steps of the open stairway. Once on the second floor, he walked down the hallway to the smallest of the four bedrooms, which he'd converted into a home office. He checked his answering machine messages and returned a few phone calls. With those tasks out of the way, he reclined in his black leather desk chair and stared unseeing at his neatly arranged bulletin board. His thoughts came back around to Melody.

What do I do now, Lord? Luke supposed he could just ask her out on a date like any normal single male; however, he sensed it wasn't the way to go about endearing Melody to him. From what she'd told him, Melody had "been there, done that." She didn't need another date. She needed a—*a hero*.

Well, I've been patient this long, Luke decided, reaching for his hand-held daily planner. *I can certainly wait some more.*

ન

Melody arrived home from work on Friday afternoon and discovered Bonnie in the kitchen. They didn't speak; Bonnie hadn't said more than three words to Melody in the past couple of days.

Mel flipped through the mail and then, unable to ignore the clanging of pans, she glanced at her sister. "Are you cooking supper tonight?"

"Mmm-hmm."

"Is Scott coming over?"

Bonnie banged a mixing bowl on the counter. "What's it to you?"

Okay, we're up to seven words, eight if I count "Mmm-hmm."

Mel gazed into Bonnie's fuming countenance, deciding she'd never seen her sister so mad. "I didn't mean anything by it. I asked because if you're cooking for Scott, I'll find something else to do and leave you two alone."

"Mom and Dad will be here. We'll hardly be *alone*."

"Fine." Melody dropped the stack of envelopes back onto the kitchen table. "Just don't count on me being here tonight for dinner."

"Fine," Bonnie repeated in a huff.

Mel left the kitchen and proceeded upstairs. She wished her parents would intervene in this ugliness between her and Bonnie. But it seemed Scott had Mom charmed and Dad confused.

Entering her bedroom, Mel told herself she didn't care anymore—she just wished she really felt that way.

Once she'd changed into blue jeans and a sweater, she pulled her cell phone from her purse and walked out onto the back porch. The sun felt warm, but the temperature had only reached the midforties. However, a lifetime of living in Wisconsin had thickened Mel's blood and the brisk late afternoon air didn't bother her.

She sat down on one of the two lawn chairs, kicked up her feet, and dialed several friends' numbers. Two had dates, one had the flu, and a couple of others weren't home.

Great. Nowhere to run and nothing to do.

At that moment, Mel saw Luke's SUV turn into the alley. She wondered if he had plans—oh, of course he did! He probably had a date. Maybe he had asked Mystery Girl out to dinner.

No, on second thought, he probably hadn't.

Melody lifted her feet off the railing and leaned forward. Luke was a puzzle. He was a special guy. Handsome. Caring. She couldn't understand why he didn't let Mystery Girl know of his interest—unless Mystery Girl had a steady boyfriend.

Mel snapped her fingers. *Then it's got to be Alicia Sims.*

Luke emerged from the side door of his garage. He wore dark slacks, a light blue shirt, and a coordinating tie. Over one shoulder he carried a large leather attaché and over the other, he'd flung his suit jacket. As he made his way up the walkway, he flicked his gaze toward the porch. Seeing Melody sitting there, he stopped.

"Hi," he said.

Melody smiled. "Hi, Luke."

"I haven't seen you in a few days. How're you doing?"

"Okay, I guess. How 'bout yourself?"

"Terrific."

Maybe he did have a date after all.

"Got any plans for tonight?"

Luke tipped his dark head. "Nothing concrete. What about you?"

"No." Melody stared at her cell phone. "I'm actually looking for something to do."

"How does dinner and a Brewers baseball game sound?"

Melody smiled and looked back at Luke. "Great. Who's all going?"

"Um. . ." He shifted his stance. "Just you and me at the moment. That idea was—um—just off the top of my head. But I know the Brewers are in town and playing tonight."

Melody felt a twinge of discomfort. Dinner and attending a baseball game alone with Luke sounded an awful lot like a date. Then again, it sure beat sitting around here all night and listening to Bonnie and Mom make wedding plans while Scott and Dad did the male bonding thing in front of the television.

"Sure. It sounds fun. What time?"

"Really?"

"Sure, why not?" Mel wondered why he looked so shocked.

Luke glanced at his watch. "Give me a half hour."

"You got it."

She watched him walk the rest of the way to his house, pull out his keys, and let himself inside. That odd feeling came over her again. *A date with Luke Berringer. . . What if someone from church sees us, and it gets around?*

It was then that Mel put two and two together. Luke probably hoped the word would spread because then Alicia would hear about it and if she had any feelings for him at all, they'd surface one way or another.

Yessiree, that Luke was a crafty guy. *Those quiet types usually are.*

Mel stood and reentered her bedroom. She wasn't thrilled about it, but she'd play along because she had grown fond of her neighbor. He'd been a good friend to her last weekend.

Besides, if he and Alicia got together, maybe she'd end up a bridesmaid in their wedding, too!

nine

I think it's shameful how you're using Luke!"

"What?" Melody whirled around and faced her sister. She had been about to climb into bed when Bonnie spouted off that ridiculous remark. "I'm not 'using' Luke. What are you talking about?"

Bonnie raised her chin. "It's obvious you're jealous, and you're using Luke to try to get what Scott and I have together."

Mel rolled her eyes. "*Whatever!* For your information, Luke and I are just friends and *he* asked me out Friday night. He's also the one who asked me to that wedding yesterday. Some guy he works with got married, and Luke didn't want to go by himself."

Bonnie put her hands on her slender hips. "And what about this morning?"

"What about it? I sat with Luke in church. So?"

Melody climbed into bed, trying to tamp down the bitterness she felt. How could Bonnie accuse her of using Luke in such a manipulative and selfish way?

"Sarah said she thinks you're jealous of me. I'm your little sister, and you're mad because I'm getting married first."

"Sarah needs to get a life."

Bonnie shrugged out of her clothes then pulled on an oversized shirt. "Most women our age want to get married. But what's soured our situation is that I'm younger than you, and you had a crush on my fiancé."

Melody felt her emotional wounds rip open all the wider. Her friends and sister had obviously been discussing this matter behind her back.

"It wasn't a crush, Bonnie. I really believed I loved Scott." She propped herself up on an elbow, hoping her sister would finally come to understand her side of this. "I'll admit to feeling envious of you at first, but that's worn off. I want to be happy for you. It's just that I'm still hurt that you believe Scott's lies instead of me."

"He never lied."

"Yes, he did."

"No, he didn't!" Bonnie raised her voice. "But Sarah and Jamie told me—"

"What?" Melody's hold on her emotions snapped. She flung herself out of bed, battle ready. "You, Sarah, and Jamie should be praying for me instead of gossiping about me and thinking the worst!"

"Don't lay sin at our door and turn this all around on us." Bonnie's face flamed with anger. "You're the one who's at fault here."

"And how's that?"

"You're jealous and now you're using Luke."

"I am not! You're delusional!"

Bonnie jabbed a finger in Mel's direction. "Jamie said she wouldn't put it past you to try to break up Scott and me."

"No way. I've decided you two *deserve* each other!"

Bonnie tipped her head. "And just what is that supposed to mean?"

"It means. . ."

A knock sounded, and without waiting for an answer, their mother opened the bedroom door and walked in. "What is going on up here? The windows are open, and the whole neighborhood can hear you girls arguing like you're ten years old!"

Bonnie sent Mom a little pout before she whirled around and climbed into her bed on the other side of the room. She left Mel to do the explaining.

Typical, she thought, sending a glare in her sister's direction.

"Melody, I want to know what you two are bickering about."

Mom folded her arms, awaiting the explanation.

"Ask Bonnie." Mel found her jeans then pulled a T-shirt from her dresser drawer. *I am out of here!* "I'm sure you won't believe anything I have to say."

"That's not true."

Oh, yes, it is, Mel thought as she dressed. But she didn't say another word.

❧

Luke sat out on his back deck. He felt so worked up he wouldn't fall asleep if someone paid him. Not only had he spent a lot of time with Melody again this past weekend, but he also sold a house this afternoon.

Lord, I'm rejoicing....

And if he was crazy about Melody before, he was in love with her now. They'd had fun on Friday night and a good time at Bob and Sue's wedding yesterday. Even though she didn't know anyone but Luke at the reception, Melody was pleasant and chatty, and everyone she met liked her at once.

Strains of her voice wafted down to Luke's ears. He stood and walked to the edge of the wooden deck and peered up at Melody's bedroom window. The light shone through the blinds and the window was partially open. He heard Melody say something more, then Bonnie.

They're arguing.

Luke retreated to his padded lawn chair. None of his business. What's more, he'd heard enough catfights coming from the Stenson home over the years, having grown up right next door. But he really hadn't heard many disputes since the girls entered adulthood. He was apt to hear more giggling.

Well, siblings tended to have their spats. Luke couldn't even begin to count the numerous scrapes he'd had with his sister. But what troubled Luke now was that he could only guess why Melody and Bonnie were quarreling—make that *who* they were quarreling about: Scott Ramsay.

Lord, this shouldn't happen, but I know things have been brewing for over a week. . .

He mulled it over some more. It seemed to him that Bill and Ellen Stenson were still so shell-shocked from Bonnie's announcement about marrying Scott that they failed to see Melody sinking into despair. Of course, Luke knew there were two sides to every story. Nonetheless, Melody and Bonnie had always enjoyed a close relationship. Perhaps the women would hash it out and put the matter to rest once and for all. But was that possible with Ramsay in the mix?

Only by God's grace. . .

The seconds ticked by and Luke tried to tune out the bickering next door, but the sisters' voices grew louder, until all at once things quieted. Then the back porch door closed with a loud bang.

He grimaced. Silence. He began to relax. But not ten minutes later Luke saw Melody running for the carport. He stood, but before he could call out to her, Bill Stenson's voice rumbled like thunder across the backyard after her.

"Melody, come back here! Don't you leave this way!"

She didn't heed the command and, moments later her car took off out of the alley with tires squealing.

Luke's gut contracted with fear. *Oh, Lord, protect her—and everyone in her path.*

৯

Melody stepped on the accelerator and headed for the freeway. She considered seeking refuge at Grandmother Cartwright's house in Genesee Depot. Grammy enjoyed pampering and spoiling Mel as she was the only Cartwright grandchild.

She looked at the clock on the dash and realized that at this late hour, Grammy would be fast asleep.

Melody decided to just drive and see where she ended up. She pulled her car onto I-43 and headed north, ignoring the lively computerized tune her cell phone produced with incoming calls. It occurred to her that maybe she really wasn't part of the Stenson family. Maybe she'd always been the odd duck out.

Lord, I feel so alone. Life seems so unfair!

She fussed and fumed all the way to Manitowoc, then cried the rest of the distance to Green Bay. In the wee hours of the morning, she stopped for gas and found an all-night restaurant right off the interstate. She ate breakfast while reading John chapter fifteen in her Bible.

"As the Father has loved me, so have I loved you. Now remain in my love. . . . I have told you this so that my joy may be in you and that your joy may be complete."

Melody stopped reading and sipped her coffee, wondering when the last time was that she experienced true joy. Not mere happiness, but pure, unadulterated joy.

Lord Jesus, what's wrong with me?

"Greater love has no one than this, that he lay down his life for his friends. . . . You did not choose me, but I chose you. . . . This is my command: Love each other ."

Those last words gave Melody pause. Love each other? She realized then that she'd been harboring a lot of hatred—hatred spawned by Scott's lies and rejection. How could the love of God penetrate through all those destructive emotions?

As she drove back to Milwaukee, she wept some more—but not tears of self-despair; they were tears of sorrow.

God forgive me for hating Scott Ramsay. She prayed like David did in Psalm 51. *"Create in me a pure heart, O God, and renew a steadfast spirit within me."*

Her cell phone rang again. This time she answered it.

"Mel, where are you?"

Her dad didn't sound angry, just insistent. "I'm okay. I'll be home in a little while."

"That's not what I asked."

Melody expelled a weary sigh. "I'm just driving by the Port Washington exits."

"What are you doing out that way?"

"I drove around all night. I had a lot of thinking to do—thinking and conversing with God."

"Well, I'm glad for the 'conversing with God' part, but I lost a night's sleep over your *driving around*."

"You did? Why?"

"Because you're my daughter, that's why. What kind of stupid question is that?"

Mel felt her throat constrict with emotion. "It's just that—I feel like everyone's against me. It hurts so bad that you all believe Scott over me, and you think I'm a liar."

"We believe you, Mel. But your mom and I are trying to be fair to both you and Bonnie while giving Scott the benefit of the doubt."

She tossed a glance heavenward. "I hope you know you sound like a politician."

Dad didn't respond to her tart reply. "Look, I've gotta go to work, but you and I will talk tonight. Got it?"

She relented. "Got it."

"I love you, Mel."

She believed him. "Love you, too."

Bleary-eyed, Melody ended the call, and she couldn't help feeling a bit hopeful. Maybe Dad was on her side after all. Perhaps Mom would come around, too. Then Bonnie. . .

Once at home, Mel showered and changed into the light blue scrubs she wore to work. Everyone had left for their jobs, and Mel had already phoned her employer to say she'd be late. She dried her short hair, touched it up with the curling iron, and then applied a small amount of cosmetics, making sure she hid those dark circles emerging beneath her eyes.

On the way downstairs, the back doorbell rang. Mel stood on tiptoes and peered through the half-moon-shaped window.

Luke.

She opened the door, noticing his crisp white dress shirt,

multicolored striped tie and gray trousers. "Hi. What are you doing here?" She waved him inside.

"I was worried about you." He stepped into the back hall.

Mel caught a whiff of the masculine scent he wore—an Oriental, woodsy blend. "Luke, you have got to be the best-smelling real estate agent in town."

He chuckled. "Thanks."

"I have time for a quick cup of coffee. Do you?"

"Sure."

She led him into the kitchen. Luke sat down at the table.

"I was on my deck last night when I saw you take off in your car," he said. "I got really worried, especially since you didn't come home all night."

Mel turned from the coffeepot and frowned. "How do you know I didn't come home all night?"

Embarrassment crossed his features. "I kept checking your carport from my office window. Like I said, I was worried about you."

"Oh." The intense light in his eyes gave her pause. But in spite of his scrutiny, she managed to fill two mugs with coffee from the thermal pot. She set one in front of Luke and brought out the cream and sugar. "If you were on your deck, I suppose you heard Bonnie and me arguing."

"I couldn't hear what was being said, but, yeah, I heard you two."

Melody felt ashamed for her part in the squabble. From now on, she'd take the high road. She wouldn't let her emotions rule her actions.

She sipped her coffee. "I'm sorry you overheard, and I'm even more sorry for worrying you, Luke."

"I'm just glad to find you safe and sound."

"Well, I don't know about the 'sound' part." She grinned and told Luke how she'd driven up to Green Bay and back. He seemed to give great thought to her every word.

"You know," he said at last, "that's how women disappear." His voice sounded composed, although the hint of warning was unmistakable. "They take off alone, go someplace that nobody imagines they'll go, and they're never seen alive again."

"Stop it, Luke." Mel didn't appreciate the scare tactic—or whatever it was supposed to be.

He reached across the table and placed his hand on hers. "Promise me you won't take off like that again."

Mel retracted her hand. "I'm not a child, so don't treat me like one." Irked, she stood, knocking her mug. Coffee sloshed over its edge. She grabbed a napkin and sopped it up, realizing her temper had already gotten the best of her once more.

"Melody, don't be angry." Luke rose from his chair. He stepped in close to her and touched her shoulder. "I meant no offense. I just—I care about you."

Melody wondered if it was her imagination or if she'd heard tenderness in his voice as he'd spoken those last four words. Either way, her aggravation vanished.

Last night she felt as though nobody cared, but this morning God showed her that both her folks and Luke had all fretted over her welfare.

She pushed out a smile. "Thanks, Luke. I care about you, too."

A pleased-looking grin tugged at the corners of his mouth. "Then will you promise? Next time you feel like escaping for a while, you'll call me first? Doesn't matter what time of day or night it is."

Her smile grew, and she concluded Luke Berringer had to be the sweetest guy on the planet. What's more, she really believed him when he said he cared about her. He meant every word; she could tell by the expression on his face.

"All right, I promise."

ten

Do you promise?"

Melody rolled her eyes. "Yes, Dad, I promise. And if it's any consolation, Luke made me promise him the same thing. No more 'dashing off to nowhere,' as you put it."

"Good." He leaned back in the armchair and narrowed his gaze. "Luke, huh? You two have been spending a lot of time together."

From her place on the sofa in the living room, Mel shrugged and staved off a yawn. "We're just friends."

"I've been hearing that word 'friend' a lot around here lately."

"Yes, well, if you're referring to my so-called *friendship* with Scott, I'll have you know he led me to believe it was something much more."

"I know, I know." Dad lifted a hand, palm side out. "I believe you, Mel." He raked his fingers through the small thatch of hair he had left on his scalp. "I don't know why Scott would lie, or fail to remember, or whatever his problem is, but I do believe you."

"Thanks." Immediate tears flooded her eyes, a consequence of no sleep in the last twenty-four hours and a long day at work.

"Now don't cry. You know I can't stand it when you girls cry."

"Sorry. I'm overtired."

"All right. Now, about Luke."

"What about him?" Mel dabbed the corners of her eyes and wondered if Bonnie shared her opinion with their parents. "I'm not using him, if that's what you're wondering."

"Using him?" A deep frown furrowed her father's bushy, gray-streaked brows. "Why would I think that?"

Melody told him the particulars of the argument she'd had with Bonnie last night.

Dad shook his head and tossed a glance upward. "This nonsense has to stop."

"I agree, but how?"

"Well," he drawled, "I might have an answer." He sent her a dubious glance. "I did have all night to think and pray on the subject."

Melody shifted uncomfortably on the couch cushion. "I'm sorry I kept you up, Dad."

"Let's forget it. Okay, here's my idea. I say we call a truce. Whatever happened between you and Scott years ago is dead and done with. You told me you repented for any wrongdoing."

Mel nodded.

"Then God has forgiven you. 'If we confess our sins, he is faithful and just and will forgive us our sins and purify us from all unrighteousness.' "

"First John one, verse nine," Melody said, recognizing the passage of scripture her dad just recited.

"But now *you* have to forgive Scott."

"I'm working on it." She picked at a thread on her scrub pants.

"No, honey, the act of forgiveness is a decision. It's immediate, like deciding to turn on the TV. You just do it."

"I did, but memories come back to haunt me and when new incidents occur, I'm hurt all over again."

"Then it's seventy times seven, just like Christ said."

Melody knew her stepfather was right. But it seemed so much easier to talk about forgiveness than to put it into practice. Nevertheless, she bobbed out a reply.

"Good. Next, Bonnie has to quit acting so insecure. I'll talk to her. And Scott. That guy better watch his p's and q's, or he's going to feel the sting of this father's wrath—and don't smile about that, Mel."

She pressed her lips together.

"Forgiveness. Remember?"

"Yes."

"Now back to Luke."

Once more, Mel gave her father a quizzical stare.

"Why are you just friends?"

"Why?" Melody didn't get it.

"You want to get married. Luke is as eligible as bachelors come. He's a nice, decent Christian man, and—"

Melody shook off the notion. The last thing she wanted to do was fall in love with a guy who thought they were "just friends"—like Scott. Except, unlike Luke, Scott had professed his undying love for her. And she'd been too naïve to see the man for what he was.

What a liar.

"Melody?"

I have to forgive Scott.

She looked at her father, amazed at how her mind had wandered. "Um—Luke is actually interested in someone else. I guess that's why we're not anything more than friends."

"Ahh. Well, that explains it. Who is she?"

Mel shrugged. "Mystery Girl. Luke won't tell me. He said he'll feel stupid if his feelings for this person get around." Mel lifted her hands in a helpless gesture. "I've told him that women can't read minds. He's got to let his feelings be known."

Dad pursed his lips. "What'd he say to that?"

"Nothing specific except that he'd rather leave that up to the Holy Spirit. I've been trying to figure out who Mystery Girl is, and I've concluded she must already be seeing somebody and that's why Luke doesn't want to ask her out. He asks me out instead." Mel laughed and babbled on. "I told Luke that people are going to think we're dating, but apparently he doesn't care. I think it's because he wants to make his mystery girl jealous, but. . ." Mel frowned, rethinking her hypothesis. "No, on second thought, that's not Luke's style. He's really sweet and honest—a very compassionate person. I've told him about all this stuff I'm going through since Bonnie's engagement, and Luke's been so supportive. He cares for me. He's said so, and it really shows. He's a good friend."

"Melody?" Dad's sat forward and clasped his wide, calloused hands. A speculative frown creased his brows. "Let's think about this for a minute."

"Sure." Did he have an idea who Mystery Girl was? Melody perked up, poised and ready to hear it.

Then, much to her disappointment, Dad shook his head. "Never mind. I'm not getting involved, at least not at this point. I have enough trouble on my plate with Bonnie and Scott." He stood and stretched before a chuckle escaped. "I'm sure the truth will sink into *Mystery Girl's* thick head one of these days."

Dad winked and strode through the dining room, toward the kitchen.

"What*ever*." Melody should have known her father wouldn't participate in any kind of guessing game. Trivial Pursuit was a favorite pastime of hers, but Dad never enjoyed such things.

"Just remember what I said." He paused under the dining room's archway and sent her a stern look. "Forgiveness."

Melody nodded. "Right. Forgiveness."

It was the third promise she had made that day.

❧

Luke pulled into the asphalt lot of the supermarket and parked. Grocery list and coupons in hand, he exited his SUV, locked it up, and ambled in the direction of the store's entrance.

He couldn't remember the last time he went food shopping on a Saturday morning. Usually he stopped at the nearest convenience store and grabbed necessities on his way home from the office or while on the road to or from an open house. But he realized this morning, as he stared at the meager contents in his refrigerator and equally sparse cupboards, that if he wanted Melody to continue to cook for him, he'd better stock up on at least the basics. Thursday night had been a complete embarrassment. Melody offered to create a pot of spaghetti with meat sauce but had to run to the store first. She had laughed off the incident, but Luke didn't think it was so funny. He wanted everything in his house to suit her—to be perfect for her. In short, nothing would please him more if she loved his home—and him!

Melody. That girl didn't stray far from his thoughts these days. Last night she actually asked him if he wanted to go out for a fish fry. Bonnie had decided to impress her fiancé with her culinary skills again, so Melody wanted an escape. Luke had been more than happy to provide it, although it troubled him that Melody still felt such derision toward Ramsay. She announced she'd forgiven him, but Luke still sensed an undercurrent of hurt and resentment. The day Melody felt nothing for the guy would be the day, in Luke's mind, that she was really over him.

"Hey, mister, wanna buy a puppy?"

Luke ground to a halt, having nearly collided with the boy sitting in a red wagon with four squirming bundles of black and beige fur. He glanced at the lady sitting in a lawn chair two feet away and guessed she was the boy's mother.

"Ah, no thanks."

"They make good pets." The towheaded youngster held up one of the animals. The boy's blue eyes were wide with eagerness. "And they don't cost a lot."

Luke grinned. The kid was a salesman in the making. "What kind are they?"

"We're not exactly sure," the woman replied before drawing deeply on a cigarette. She was noticeably thin and wore a purple shirt and blue jeans. She'd pulled back her straight blond hair into a ponytail. "They're half golden retriever and half something else. Might be a Lab and German shepherd mix. We're not sure."

"Hmm." Luke nodded his understanding.

"Only fifty bucks," the boy said, holding up a puppy. Then he quickly tried to subdue the others before they escaped from the high-sided wagon.

Luke scratched the animal behind its soft, floppy ears.

"We're trying to sell them," the woman added. "If we don't, they'll go to the Humane Society tomorrow. I've had it. My entire house smells like puppies."

"If they go to the Humane Society, they might hafta get put to sleep," the kid added, wearing a look of remorse. "They got too many dogs there."

Luke didn't think that was true, but he admired the sales pitch. "I'm sure these little guys will sell. But I'm not interested. Thanks anyhow." He smiled and walked away.

However, as he pushed his shopping cart down the produce aisle, he thought back to what Melody said about always wanting a puppy. What if he bought her one? She could keep it at his house since her mom had allergies.

Luke stymied the grin twitching his lips. That'd be one way to lure Melody over to his house. Of course, he'd never want to appear manipulative or, worse, deceptive. On the other hand, he'd considered buying a dog on more than one occasion. He'd just never gotten around to actually doing it.

Yeah, I need a puppy like I need a hole in my head, Luke thought as he selected several tomatoes. But as he strolled up and down the food aisles, the idea gained merit. A dog would mean companionship. A dog would also be a means of protection for his property when he wasn't around. On the other hand, having a pet might infringe on his freedom. But if it didn't work out, Luke felt sure his sister Amber would take the dog. She and her husband and four kids lived in a rural area, and they loved animals.

What could he lose?

Luke found the dog food aisle and heaved a bag formulated for puppies into his grocery cart.

I must be nuts, he thought as he checked out.

With his items bought and bagged, Luke wheeled them out to his SUV. He loaded them into the back of the vehicle and returned the cart before approaching the boy selling the puppies.

"I changed my mind. I'll buy one."

The kid looked delighted to make the sale.

"If you don't have a preference," the blond woman with the cigarette said, "I'd suggest a female. I think they're easier to train."

Luke shrugged. "Okay."

"But there's only one girl left." The youngster found her and handed the puppy to Luke.

He inspected the roly-poly, wiggling pup. Her dark eyes shone with intelligence and spunk. Her floppy ears framed a black face with caramel-colored markings that was greeting-card cute.

A mental image of Melody at eight years old trying to teach her rabbit to bark flashed through Luke's mind. He had a feeling she'd fall in love with this dog in a minute, the lucky mutt.

Luke smiled. "Sold."

eleven

Luke somehow made it home from the grocery store with a squirming, scared, ten-week-old puppy in his lap. When he pulled into the alley, he noticed the Stensons' opened garage door. As he pulled alongside his own garage and parked, he spotted Melody and her dad. With the puppy tucked under his arm, he walked next door.

"Hey, look what I got." Luke laughed when he saw Melody's eyes light up.

"Oh, how cute!" She hopped off the ladder on which she'd been perched. "Where'd you get him—or her?"

"Her, and I just bought her from a kid selling puppies at the grocery store."

"She's adorable."

Luke allowed Melody to take the puppy, and she enfolded the animal in her arms.

"You are so sweet," she murmured to the dog. The puppy responded by chewing on the collar of her forest green, short-sleeved polo shirt.

Luke noticed Bill Stenson watching them intently.

"I've been thinking of getting a dog," Luke began in a lame way, "but now that I actually purchased one, I'm doubting my sanity."

Melody grinned. "I'll help you train her. When I was a kid, I read countless books on how to train dogs. I wanted a puppy so badly. . . ."

Bill rolled his eyes and returned to sanding the four-drawer dresser he'd been working on. The thing had been painted a gaudy red, and Luke guessed Mel's dad planned to refurbish the piece.

Luke returned his focus to Melody. "In all honesty, I hoped you'd say you'd help me."

"Oh, I will." She nuzzled the puppy.

"I figure if it doesn't work out, Amber will take the dog. I'm planning to spend July Fourth with my sister and her family anyhow."

"No, Luke, you can't get rid of her. Look how lovable she is!" Melody kissed the top of the dog's head. "She'll be a good girl, *won't you, sweetheart?*"

Bill stopped sanding long enough to send Luke a skeptical glance.

"Can I show my mom and Bonnie?"

Luke turned back to Melody. "Sure."

She headed for the side door of the garage.

"Hey." Bill halted her in midstride. "Don't take that dog in the house or your mother will be in the emergency room all afternoon."

"I won't."

"And you'll have to keep your clothes separate from ours and do your own wash if you're going to be training that puppy."

"I wash my own clothes anyway. But, yes, Dad, I'll be careful. And I'll just show Mom and Bonnie the puppy through the screen door." Melody turned back to Luke. "What's her name?"

"I haven't named her yet."

"Oh." She glanced at the puppy then back at Luke. "Can I help you name her, too?"

Luke couldn't see why not. He nodded. "Yeah."

"Cool. You're awesome." After giving him a smile that took his breath away, she left the garage.

Luke's heart swelled in his chest, threatening to burst.

Bill stopped rubbing the sandpaper over the painted wood. "I'm thinking Mel's going to be spending a lot of time over at your place, what with helping you train that new dog."

Luke walked over to where Bill Stenson stood. "Is that all right with you?"

Bill replied with a single incline of his head. "But I trust you to be a gentleman at all times, Luke."

"Yes, sir. I wouldn't dream of being anything less."

"Good." Bill plugged in his electric sander while eyeing Luke. "I get the impression that you're romantically interested in Mel. Am I right?"

Luke was momentarily thrown off guard by the blunt question. "Mr. Stenson, I think I've loved Melody since we were in fourth grade."

He chuckled. "Well, I know Mel thinks highly of you. She told me she cares for you. Guess that's a good start."

Luke already knew that; Melody had said as much, but he wanted so much more. "Honestly, Mr. Stenson—"

"Call me Bill. It's not like you're just a neighbor kid anymore."

"Okay. *Bill*." Luke grinned and shifted his stance. He cleared his throat. "I'm praying for two things. One is that Jesus will be Melody's first love and, two, that I'll be her second." He paused. "Make that three things I'm praying for." He paused, weighing his words with care. "I'm praying Melody will get Scott Ramsay out of her system once and for all."

Bill nodded and his expression said he understood. "Your third request is well on its way to being answered. We had a family meeting and Scott was in on it. We talked about forgiving and forgetting and moving on."

"Glad to hear it." Luke, however, wasn't convinced Melody's emotions were so neatly packaged and ready to be stowed.

"We're one big happy family again, much to my relief." Bill sighed.

Luke offered a perfunctory smile.

"And Mel's made up with her girlfriends."

"Yes, I did hear about that."

"But. . ." Bill cocked a brow. "Mel thinks you're interested in someone else. Some *mystery girl.*"

Luke hooted and shook his head. "Okay, I'll admit it. I've got a ways to go before I get the message through to her. But at least she's now aware I exist."

"Who's now aware you exist?" Melody asked, reentering the garage. She carried the puppy in the crook of her arm like a baby.

"None of your beeswax," Bill retorted while Luke stood by feeling somewhat mortified. He'd never intended for Melody to overhear their conversation. He should have been more careful. "This is man talk," Bill continued, "and not for your tender, female ears."

"Oh, Dad. . ." Melody threw an annoyed glance upward, but her gaze came back to rest on Luke. He saw the questions gathering like storm clouds in her sky-blue eyes.

No way around it, he'd have some explaining to do later.

❧

Melody felt her face warm with an indignant flame. How could Luke share his secret with Dad, but not her? Did Luke think she was a blabbermouth? Well, she wasn't!

Seconds later, reason returned, and Mel wondered if her father had been the one to broach that topic. After all, Mel had told Dad about Luke's mystery girl. Perhaps he had pressed Luke on the subject.

"I—um—have to pick up supplies for the dog," Luke said, and Mel heard the hesitancy in his voice. "I also have groceries to unpack."

She arched her brows. "You bought groceries?"

"Yeah." Luke smiled and Mel thought he looked relieved. "So will you—um—come to the pet store with me?"

She cast aside the feeling that she'd been slighted and made a mental note to ask Luke about Mystery Girl later. "Sure, I'll come along. We can bring Lexus with us. I hear they allow dogs in the store."

"Lexus?" Now it was Luke's turn to raise his brows.

Melody felt herself blush. "Do you think that name suits her?" She glanced down at the now sleeping puppy in her arms. "Think of a sleek black car with tan leather upholstery—that's what this puppy's coloring reminds me of."

"I think of a Mercedes Benz." Dad's guffaw filled the garage.

Melody rolled her eyes. "You can't holler 'Mercedes' out the back door." She turned to Luke. "But you could call 'Lexi,' short for *Lexus*."

Luke pursed his lips and mulled it over. "Lexi's a cute name."

Melody smiled.

They left the garage for Luke's house. He carried in the grocery bags, and Melody helped him unpack the food. The puppy awoke and nosed her way in between Mel's ankles.

"I can't believe you bought all this stuff," she said, eyeing the bags of flour, sugar, brown sugar, bottles of various spices, and packs of ground beef, chicken, and pork chops. He'd even purchased a gallon of milk, nondairy creamer, and sticks of butter. "It's about time."

Luke chuckled. "Yeah, I guess every couple of years I need to stock up."

"Every *couple of years*?" Mel laughed, deciding Luke needed a wife in the worst way.

Well, at least he had a puppy now. She supposed that was a start.

twelve

Melody didn't have any other plans on this gorgeous last day of April, so accompanying Luke to the pet store gave her something to do. She held Lexi in her lap as they drove the distance in Luke's SUV. The store was animal-friendly, so taking a pet inside wasn't an issue. Then, while he purchased a dog crate and other supplies, Mel spoke with the store manager and learned several new things about housebreaking and training a puppy.

On the way back home, Luke muttered that dogs were expensive.

Melody laughed and cuddled Lexi. Minutes later, he turned into the alley and parked in his garage. Mel grabbed one of the many shopping bags. As she walked toward his house, her father hailed her from the other side of the fence.

"How 'bout you two plan to eat with us tonight? Bonnie's not cooking." Dad grinned. "I'm getting tired of eating that gourmet slop that she's been trying to impress Scott with, so I'm grilling burgers."

"Yum." Mel set Lexi on the grass.

"Sounds good to me, too." Luke's voice resounded from behind her, and Melody peered over her shoulder at him. His arms were full of pet equipment, so she stepped off the sidewalk and let him pass.

"Will it be just the four of us?" Mel asked.

Her father shook his balding head. "No, Bonnie and Scott will be here. So we'll be six altogether."

Melody felt a heavy frown settle over her features. She couldn't pinpoint it, but there was something troubling about Scott

Ramsay—something that caused Mel to doubt his sincerity, and even his faith.

Her dad narrowed his gaze as if he divined her thoughts. "Forgiveness, remember?"

"Yeah, yeah, yeah."

Dad gave her one of his hard stares before inclining his head. "That puppy is escaping, Mel."

She sucked in a breath of alarm before running after Lexi. Mel caught her before she disappeared around the far side of Luke's garage.

"Some baby-sitter you are," her dad teased.

Melody sent him a dismissive wave and walked into Luke's house. She found him sitting on the kitchen floor assembling Lexi's new crate. It was a cream-colored, hard plastic model with plenty of air vents and a sturdy grated-metal door that clicked soundly into place.

"Doggy jail," Luke said with a laugh, pushing the thing under his kitchen table.

"No, it's her *bed*." Melody shook her head at him. "If you get me some old linens, I'll make a nice, soft place for Lexi to sleep."

Luke stood, left the kitchen, and minutes later returned with some well-worn towels and mismatched sheets that had obviously seen better days.

"Perfect." Melody arranged the bedding, then set the puppy in the crate, and closed the door. "Nap time."

Luke chuckled and offered Melody his hand. She took it and he helped her up off the floor.

At that very moment, Bonnie and Scott burst in through the side door unannounced.

"Okay, what are you guys doing?" Bonnie set her hands on her slender hips. A smile tugged at her watermelon-pink mouth. "Dad sent us over here to spy."

Melody laughed and withdrew her hand from Luke's. "Yeah,

sure he did. He probably wanted to get rid of the two of you for a while."

"You know, Mellow, I think you're right about that one." Scott flashed her one of his movie star smiles before sauntering over to Luke.

The men shook hands in greeting.

Melody stifled a grimace. Every time Scott called her "Mellow" she wanted to smack him.

"Actually," Bonnie said, "Scott and I have business to discuss with Luke."

"Want me to leave?" Mel suddenly relished the idea.

"No, stay. It's all right." Bonnie's blue-eyed gaze settled on Luke. "Can we sit down and talk?"

He nodded. "Let's move into the living room."

Mel followed her sister and the two men through the dining area and into Luke's comfortable living room. In the past couple of weeks, she learned about the extensive remodeling Luke had done on this place after his folks died. It made her appreciate everything from the paint and varnish to the expanded living room. What's more, since she started hanging out over here, Mel had begun to feel right at home, even though Luke's leather furniture was too "bachelor" for her tastes.

She plopped down on one end of the couch and folded her legs beneath her. To her shock and horror, Scott seated himself right beside her. He put an arm around her and hugged her shoulders.

"So how's my little sis on this fine Saturday afternoon?"

Melody gave in to her instincts and elbowed him in the ribs, but not quite as hard as she would have liked. Even so, Scott fell over onto the empty side of the sofa, feigning injury.

He's trying to be funny, Mel told herself. However, Scott's antics only caused her to dislike him all the more.

And this wasn't the first time he'd done something stupid, either. The night of their family meeting, Scott had sneaked up on Melody as she loaded the dishwasher. Placing his hands at her waist, he'd tickled her. Mel's parents and sister were still sitting at the dining room table and had, of course, heard the shriek that followed. Scott just laughed and announced that Melody "spooked easily." But it was Melody who'd received the cold stare from Bonnie and the look of reproof from her folks. Scott had a way of making her appear the guilty one, the instigator.

After discussing the matter at great length with Luke, Melody concluded she'd lost her parents' trust when they learned she hadn't told them about dating Scott. It hadn't been like her, not in her character, to keep anything from them. Now Mom and Dad probably felt like they didn't really know her. Perhaps they wondered what else she hadn't told them, and Melody could visualize her mother wondering if maybe Bonnie's accusations had merit.

Melody glanced at her sister now. From her place in the overstuffed, tan leather armchair, Bonnie wore a tight, polite little grin. But when Melody glanced across the way at Luke, he replied with an assuring wink as if to let her know he was on her side.

She smiled at him. What would she ever do without a friend like Luke?

"I'm going to make some coffee." Mel stood and headed for the kitchen. She backtracked, eyeing Luke. "Did you buy coffee this morning?"

He scrunched up his face. "No, I forgot."

Melody laughed. "Okay, I'll run next door and get some."

She took her time about it and even stayed in Luke's pristine kitchen while the coffee brewed. Lexi slept, curled up, in the corner of her crate.

Once the coffeemaker finished its gurgling and sputtering, Melody pulled four mugs from the cupboard. Next, she fished out a black lacquer tray that Luke kept in the lower cabinet;

Mel had seen it there along with his pots and pans. Dishcloth in hand, she wiped off the thin layer of dust and swallowed a giggle, wondering when the tray was last used. Placing the coffeepot and mugs on its shining surface, she opened the fridge and found the nondairy creamer. Luke's sugar bowl was in use again, too, ever since he returned from the store this morning. Mel set the condiments onto the tray as well. Then she strode back into the living room.

Luke saw her coming and made room for her on the love seat. Bonnie still sat in the armchair, but Scott had stretched out on the sofa. His leather penny loafers dangled over the armrest.

"Just make yourself at home, Scott. Don't be shy." Mel couldn't resist the quip as she sat down and began pouring coffee.

Scott chuckled.

Bonnie cleared her throat. "As I was saying—"

"Sure, I'd be happy to show you and Scott the house," Luke injected.

Melody looked at her sister then at Luke. "What house?"

"The old Thornton place." Luke sipped his coffee.

Mel fought the urge to gape. "The Thorntons' place?" The reply really hadn't warranted repeating, but Mel was battling shock.

"Scott and I are interested in buying it," Bonnie explained as she crossed the room and helped herself to a cup of java. She added a splash of creamer. "Scott and I saw the FOR SALE sign out in front and just fell in love with it."

But I've loved that old Victorian home ever since I can remember! Melody fought to control her envy.

"Like I said. . ." Luke sat back in the settee. "The property needs a lot of work."

"Oh, but it'll be fun to fix it up." Bonnie walked back to the armchair, looking Scott's way. "Right, honey?"

"Anything you say, babe."

Honey? Babe? Melody wanted to gag. But instead she pretended to be unaffected by this latest turn of events. She fixed her coffee then scooted back on the love seat, folding one leg beneath her. She forced herself to act friendly and impervious in spite of her heart screaming, *It's just not fair!*

The Thorntons' house. It was located two blocks away and stood in regal splendor overlooking the northwest Milwaukee neighborhood. Melody figured it must have been one of the first homes built in this section of the city, and it had always been her dream to live in it someday.

But now her sister would live in it.

The last precious piece of her dream shattered.

Melody felt like sobbing. Everything she had always dreamed of and longed for in life, a beautiful wedding, a handsome groom, her dream home, was being handed to Bonnie.

Lord, this is so not fair!

❧

Later that afternoon, Melody kept silent throughout dinner. But the stress of the situation overcame her, and she polished off two hamburgers, a lumberjack-sized portion of her mother's potato salad, and a homemade fudge brownie. She figured at this rate she'd weigh five hundred pounds by the time Bonnie and Scott's wedding day rolled around.

When the meal ended, Mom and Bonnie strolled into the kitchen and talked bridal gowns while they washed dishes. Dad and Scott ambled into the den, but Luke declined the offer to sit with the guys and surf the cable channels.

"Maybe we should check on Lexi," Mel suggested. She suddenly yearned for a reason to escape the matrimony chatter, and she wasn't about to sit in the den with her dad and Scott.

"Great idea."

Melody called a farewell to her folks before following Luke to his place.

"I'm so-o-o full," she complained as he let them in through his side entrance.

He chuckled. "I was just going to ask: What's eating you? No pun intended."

Lexi whined in her crate and Melody snapped to attention. She rushed to the crate and carried the dog outside where Lexi did her business.

"Success!"

Returning to the kitchen Luke grinned at the small victory. He folded his arms across the periwinkle golf shirt he wore. "Now back to my question." He narrowed his gaze. "What's up?"

Melody shrugged. She knew what Luke meant. He evidently had sensed her inner turmoil during dinner. But where did she begin?

She sighed. "Same old stuff."

"It upsets you when Scott's around?"

Again, she lifted her shoulders in uncertainty.

"Maybe you do have feelings for him after all."

"Oh, I have feelings for him, all right." Mel couldn't keep the cynicism out of her voice. "Irritation, aggravation, and annoyance are the top three."

Luke laughed. "Did you want to think about that for a minute?"

Melody smiled at the comeback and sat on the cool tiled floor. She pulled Lexi into her arms. "I think it's obvious how I feel about Scott. I dislike him. I have absolutely no respect for him." She exhaled audibly. "I'm not a person who can hide her emotions."

"So I've discovered."

"Then why did you ask if I still have feelings for him—and I assume you meant romantic feelings?"

"Just making sure, I guess." Luke sat down on the floor across from Mel. The puppy wiggled out of her grasp and bounded over to her new owner. She jumped into his lap, biting his hands and anything else she could sink her teeth into. Luke reached for one of the chew toys he'd purchased today and distracted Lexi, who obviously wanted to play. "I could tell something's been bothering you all afternoon."

"You're right."

"So what is it?"

Melody gave in, sensing Luke wouldn't be satisfied until she bared her soul—as she often did of late. "Luke, ever since I was a little girl I've fantasized about living in the Thorntons' house. I imagined myself a sort of urban princess, serving tea in the parlor to my guests. I didn't even know the place was for sale, not that I could afford to buy it or anything. But the fact that Bonnie wants it, and will most likely get it, is like another knife in my heart."

Luke pursed his lips, mulling it over. "Have you ever walked through the Thorntons' house?"

Mel shook her head.

"Hmm. Well, as you know, the Thorntons were an elderly couple—"

"Ancient, you mean. They were 'elderly' when we were kids."

Luke chuckled. "Well, yeah, I guess that's true. Anyway, as they aged Mr. and Mrs. Thornton refused to relocate, even after they required assisted living arrangements. So a nephew moved in and took care of them, although I cringe when I imagine what kind of care they received. Ron Pittman is the relative who inherited the house. He contacted our office, and I did a market analysis for him. When I did my initial walk-through, I was appalled by filth. The guy's a total slob."

Melody wrinkled her nose, imagining the sight.

"The place is a lot better now. Pittman moved out and hired a company to clean it up. But it's still in rough shape." Luke set the puppy on the floor then stood. He held out his hand to Mel. "Come on. I'll give you your own private tour." He smiled before adding, "*Princess Melody.*"

thirteen

Luke punched in the pass code to the lock fitted over the knob, and the back door opened. A musty, rotten odor assailed Mel's senses as she entered the spacious hallway. She noticed the cracks on the plastered walls that were painted a drab green color.

Luke grabbed a black flashlight hooked on a nail to his right and flipped on its switch.

"We'll start in the basement. Come on."

He led the way to the winding stairs.

"Watch your step."

He offered Mel his hand and she took it, thinking that each time her fingers met his palm she enjoyed the sensation more and more.

"There's no electricity down here, and if you'll notice there's a dirt floor and stone foundation."

"Is it crumbling?" Mel strained to see. It was dusk outside, but dark as pitch down here in the basement.

"I think someone tried to plaster over the stone, and that's what's coming off now."

"Oh." She glanced around then wove her fingers between Luke's and decided not to let him too far out of her reach. "It's creepy down here."

In the glow of the flashlight, she saw him grin at her. "You're not the kind of female who screams at the sight of spiders, are you?"

"No."

"Didn't think so."

"Just snakes. Big snakes, like the ones they show on the

Discovery Channel or Animal Planet."

Luke laughed. "We're not likely to run into any of those down here."

He showed her the fruit and wine cellars, where the water heater and the monstrosity of a furnace were located.

"The furnace needs to be replaced." Luke stated the obvious. "I wouldn't be surprised if it was the original."

"Can we get out of here? I think I've seen enough of this dungeon."

Luke chuckled but shined the beam of light toward the stairwell. Melody ran up the steps and waited for him in the hallway. She watched as Luke flicked several switches at the top of the basement stairs and overhead lights went on.

"I'll show you the kitchen now."

Melody followed him up another short flight of stairs. He opened shuttered doors to reveal a washer and dryer.

"The utility room," he said.

"I'd say it's more like a closet with appliances shoved inside."

"Yeah, that's about it." Luke closed the door and turned on the kitchen lights.

Melody gaped at her primitive surroundings. Pea green rubber tile covered the floor. A white enamel-coated cast-iron sink from the 1940s occupied most of the far wall. A relic of a range stood against another, its oven door askew. There were no cupboards and no counters, no dishwasher, and the space in which a refrigerator should stand appeared useless. No refrigerator on the market today would fit in there.

"How did Mrs. Thornton prepare any meals?"

"Probably used her kitchen table like you'd use counter space."

"Mmm."

"My suggestion to prospective buyers is that they knock out this wall here." He led Melody around to the pantry where four wide, long shelves ran the length of the wall with cabinets underneath them. "This would enlarge the kitchen and then cupboards could be installed."

"Yeah, I guess that would work."

The tour continued, and Luke walked her through the large dining room. Despite its gaudy red and gold wallpaper, it showed promise. But the living room or "parlor" was smaller than the average bedroom. However, across the hardwood floor in the foyer there was another "sitting room" of equal size.

"Tell me what you think so far."

Melody turned and faced him. "This house is proof that looks are deceiving. From the outside this place seems like it would be a charming Victorian home. But the inside is so—so awful, it'll send the best do-it-yourselfer screaming into the night."

Luke appeared amused by her assessment. "Let's go upstairs."

Mel trailed him to the winding staircase. At first glance, it looked like a mahogany grandeur, but it creaked eerily with each step they took.

"This staircase is safe, isn't it?" Mel grasped the intricately carved but rickety railing. No help there.

"The inspector said it was safe."

Mel heard the grin in Luke's voice. "Are you laughing at me?"

"A little." Luke's tone grew serious. "Melody, I'd never lead you into harm's way. Don't you know better than that?"

"Well, yeah, but it never hurts to ask." The wood moaned in protest beneath her foot, and she hesitated to go further.

Luke turned back and offered his hand. Mel took it; his grip felt strong and sure, unlike the wobbly railing.

"You're perfectly safe," he assured her.

Mel believed him and her misgivings seemed to evaporate.

They reached the second floor, and Mel discovered it had four bedrooms and one good-sized bathroom. The only trouble was, none of the bedrooms had closets and the plumbing in the bathroom appeared to be as old and outdated as the ancient furnace.

As they rode back to Luke's place, Melody retreated into contemplative silence. Luke, too, seemed consumed with his thoughts.

"You know what?" she said sometime later as they sat outside on Luke's back deck. "The Thornton place is sort of like my infatuation was with Scott years ago. On the outside it looked romantic and wonderful, like a dream come true. I mean, I sure thought so. But I never looked inside, at the real relationship, where the problems were hidden. That would be kind of like buying that old wreck without seeing the inside, naïvely believing I was getting my dream house."

"Spoken like a true English major."

She grinned and kicked up her heels, placing her feet on the wooden rail. "I suppose that's a weird analogy, but it sort of goes along with my girlish dreams."

Melody glanced at Luke. His puppy slept on his chest and with one hand he methodically stroked the animal's soft fur. It made Mel tired just watching him.

She stifled a yawn.

"I'm sorry you've had your dreams dashed."

She heard the note of compassion in his voice, and it made her wish she were Lexi, being held close to Luke's heart.

"But just remember—where dreams end, hope begins."

Melody thought it over and smiled. "That's really nice, Luke. *Where dreams end, hope begins.* I'm impressed. That's rather poetic."

He chuckled.

She lazed back in the cushioned chair and studied his profile. She could see it clearly, thanks to the yard light and the glow of the streetlamps in the alley. His shadowy jawline, the contour of his cheek, the way his walnut-colored hair was neatly trimmed around his ear. . . His slightly crooked nose with its bump at the bridge—due to kickball game injury in the seventh grade. . . Melody still recalled the buzz around school when Luke Berringer broke his nose.

Then suddenly his gaze met hers and Melody looked away. She felt embarrassed to have been caught staring at him. She couldn't imagine what was wrong with her tonight. Her thoughts were all askew. She and Luke were friends. Just friends.

"Hey, Melody, can I ask you something personal?"

She swallowed her sudden discomfort. "Sure."

"How come you don't sing anymore—you know, solo in church, rejoin the choir? You have such a pretty singing voice."

"Thanks." She had to laugh. "It's funny you ask me that. My dad and I were discussing this very topic right before you showed up to introduce your new puppy."

Luke wore a little smile along with an expectant expression.

"Why don't I sing like I used to?" She gazed out over Luke's backyard. "I guess it goes along with the whole forgiveness thing."

What Melody didn't add was that she used to sing to Scott. Her love for him had put the song of joy in her heart. When he dumped her, she felt like something died inside. "I don't know. Maybe God took my gift away."

"Hmm." Luke seemed to mull it over. "I heard you sing last week when I sat next you in church, and your gift sounded pretty good to me."

Mel smiled at the compliment, and it occurred to her then that in grade school and high school the object of her song was Jesus. Somehow in college, the show of affection had gotten transferred to Scott.

"Listen, you can sing in my ear anytime."

Melody laughed, but felt flattered all the same. "Thanks, Luke. You have a way of encouraging me. Maybe I'll—I'll think about joining choir again."

"Good." He sent her a grin before glancing at his gold-tone wristwatch. Then he stood. "Ten o'clock news is on. Want to come in and watch it with me?"

"I suppose. . ." Melody lifted her heels off the rail then pushed to her feet. "You're a news junkie, you know that? You watch cable news, local news, news magazine shows—"

"I know it." He heaved a dramatic sigh. "It's an incurable habit, I'm afraid."

"Well, there is hope," Melody said, entering the house while Luke held the door for her. "I did catch you watching a sports channel the other night."

He chuckled, and they made their way to the kitchen. Luke set the puppy in her crate and closed the door before walking the rest of the way into the living room. He collapsed into the far side of the love seat and lifted the remote, turning on his wide-screen television.

Melody ambled in behind him and without giving it much thought, she plopped down next to him. She'd left plenty of room between them, but it still felt too cozy for *just friends*.

Suddenly Melody was very much aware of Luke Berringer— and not as the shy, geeky guy she'd known most of her life, but as a handsome, *single* man.

Lord, my mind is going haywire, here. What's the matter with me?

A commercial aired on TV, and Luke picked up the remote and pressed the MUTE button.

Luke cleared his throat. "Hey, listen. I've—um—wanted to explain about this morning. And it just never seemed like the right time—until now."

In an instant Mel knew what he meant. "About sharing your secret with my dad?" She shook her head and gave the topic a dismissive wave. "Don't worry about it. I told my father that you're in love with some mystery girl, and—"

"Melody, I'm not *in love* with anyone else," Luke said, cupping her chin, urging her gaze to his.

"I—I guess I didn't mean love, exactly." Melody felt oddly uncomfortable at the moment. "I meant—*interested*."

Luke rolled his eyes and sat back on the love seat.

And then it dawned on Melody.

"You're embarrassed! Is that why you won't tell me who this woman is?"

He grinned and flicked his gaze in her direction. "Let's just drop it, okay?"

That's it. Melody concealed a smug smile. She still had a hunch that Alicia Sims was aka Mystery Girl.

As they sat there in silence, a weird kind of sadness coiled its way around Mel's insides. Mystery Girl didn't know how lucky she was!

Luke crossed his leg, ankle to knee, and un-muted the television. Melody felt as though he had somehow inflated his existence because not quite an inch remained between them.

She stared at the TV, paying little to no attention to what the anchorman reported. All she could think about was how much she'd enjoy scooting in a bit closer to Luke.

And that's a great way to ruin a perfect relationship—fall in love with a friend.

Melody stood. "I'd better go home. I have things to do before church tomorrow."

"Like what?" Luke wore a mischievous expression.

"Like laundry," Mel quipped.

He chuckled and rose from the love seat. "I'll walk you out."

"Don't bother."

"I insist."

Melody replied with a careless shrug, but she failed to hide her grin as they walked to the kitchen.

"Wait a sec. I want to give you something."

Luke crossed the room and opened a drawer. He extracted a brass-colored key connected to a large round ring and tossed it to her. Mel caught it with little effort.

"What's this?"

"The key to my heart."

"Honestly, Luke." Mel laughed at his feeble jest, wondering

how he could spout such nonsense with a straight face.

"Actually," Luke informed her, "it's the key to my house. Might come in handy if I'm not home, and Lexi has to go out." He paused and regarded her for a moment. "You're still willing to help me train her, aren't you?"

"Of course." Mel slipped the key ring onto her wrist like a bracelet. "In fact, I was going to ask if you wanted me to come by and let her out on my lunch breaks. I get a whole hour, and I work just minutes away."

"That would be great. Thanks, Melody."

She gave him a smile. "No problem. What are friends for?"

But as she left Luke's place and made her way home, she had to admit her last comment belied the feelings in her heart.

Friends. She wouldn't mind if their relationship became much more. However, the realization was frightening. It couldn't happen again, falling for a guy who didn't love her in return.

Determination replaced the disappointment and trepidation mounting inside her. Melody wouldn't let it happen!

Opening the side door of the house, she let herself in and tried to mentally rewire her short-circuiting brain.

We're friends. Luke and I are just friends.

fourteen

For the next ten days, Melody did her best to avoid Luke. She decided putting some distance between them wouldn't be a bad idea. But it didn't work, and she found herself wondering if Luke had built-in radar. Mel scheduled her lunch hour at different times, but he always managed to show up while she let Lexi outside, and he often brought lunch for the both of them. On some days Mel dawdled home after work, hoping Luke would get to the puppy first so she wouldn't have to go over and let her out. He didn't. Other afternoons she rushed home so she'd finish caring for Lexi before he arrived, but Luke always managed to be home when she got there.

Her plans failed on all accounts. Worse, Mel couldn't seem to get herself to turn down Luke's offers for dinner or a walk with the puppy or even a chat on his back deck. Her parents were fond of him. In fact, they had always had liked and respected Luke, but now that he and Mel were good friends, they encouraged him to come around. Dad even invited him to spend Mother's Day with the family, which Luke did, and Mom blushed to her blond hairline when Luke brought her flowers and candy. Mel felt proud that he outdid Scott whose name only appeared on the card and gift that Bonnie purchased for their mother. Moreover, with Luke nearby, the holiday was tolerable—actually pleasurable for Melody.

But, in a word, she felt *doomed*. The more time she spent with Luke, the more time she wanted to spend with him.

Mel was only too glad when Darla and Max's wedding day neared. As one of the bridesmaids, Mel was soon caught up in final dress fittings, bridal showers, and last-minute preparations. She was forced to take a sabbatical from puppy training; however, Luke's friends, the Wheelers, promised to help him out.

"Hey, Mel, I need a huge favor."

She looked up from the bouquet she'd put together from wrapping bows, a memento for Darla from today's shower that the ladies at church organized.

Melody stood and smiled at her friend, the bride to be. She'd seemed so happy today, so in love with Max. But now a heavy frown marred Darla's strawberry blond brows. "Sure, what's up?"

"I just found out that my cousin and her husband—you know, the two who agreed to sing the duet at my wedding. . ."

Melody nodded in spite of the immediate feeling of impending disaster clenching her stomach.

"Both have strep throat and laryngitis. They can't talk, let alone sing, and my wedding is two weeks away!"

"Oh, they'll be fine by then."

Darla shook her head, and then her hazel eyes filled with tears. "They canceled on me."

"Two weeks is a long time." Melody sensed what was coming, and she fought down the panic. "Laryngitis doesn't last that long."

"But what if it does? My cousin is right. We can't take chances. I have to find two more singers—"

"No! No! No!" Mel wagged her head. "I won't do it. I can't. I just can't sing anymore."

"Yes, you can." Darla looked stricken. "I called Max, and he phoned Luke who said he'd sing the duet if you would."

Mel raised her brows. "Asking me was Luke's idea?"

"No, it was mine. I thought of the two of you right away, and Luke's already agreed to it."

Melody studied her friend's expression and decided she wasn't fibbing. But in the next moment, she wanted to laugh at the irony. "No, I am *not* singing a love song with Luke Berringer, okay?" Melody felt sure if she did, it would be the end of her heart.

"I thought you liked Luke."

"I do, but—"

"Pleeeeeeze," Darla begged. "You're the best soprano I can think of on such short notice. And Luke's a good baritone. You'll sound terrific together."

Mel rolled her eyes and, before she could refuse yet again, Darla shoved a score into her hands.

"Just try it. Will you?" she pleaded. "My cousin wrote this song for Max and me. This is our special day, and—"

"All right. All right. You guilted me into it." Melody sighed. "I'll try out the song and see what happens, but I'm not promising anything." She sent her friend a stern glare.

"You're awesome."

"No, actually, I'm pretty rusty. I might just croak like a frog, and then what?"

"What are you talking about? You sing like an angel." A grin spread across Darla's freckled peaches-and-cream face. "Thanks."

Mel handed her the ribbons-and-bows bouquet in reply, and her friend's smile grew. Then she hugged Mel before strolling off to chat with a group of ladies. Watching her go, Melody felt the proverbial noose tightening around her neck.

≥∘

Downstairs in the fellowship hall of the church, Luke did his best to plunk out the tune on the piano. The Sunday morning service had ended, and he persuaded Melody into an initial run-through of the duet for Darla and Max's wedding.

"I'm not happy about this," she groused. She sat on the bench beside him, her arms folded tightly in front of her.

"Yeah, I can tell." He smiled and spotted a hint of a grin tugging at her pretty rose-colored mouth.

She relaxed her arms. "Luke, I can't do this. I just can't. I mean, have you read these lyrics? They're sappy. Can't Darla and Max play a tape or something?"

Luke mulled over her complaint. He didn't think the lyrics were "sappy," but he sensed Mel still wrestled with whatever roadblock held her back from singing.

Lord, tear down these strongholds. . .

He lifted his fingers off the piano keys and tried to reassure her. "Hey, listen, it's just the two of us down here. No one's going to hear us if we hit any sour notes. Let's just go over the song once and see what happens."

She pursed her lips but didn't reply.

"Close your eyes," Luke urged her, "and imagine Darla and Max at the altar. They've just spoken their vows. . ."

Luke started to play again. The composer indicated the male voice went first, so he sang:

"Come now, my love, and take my hand,

"As we stand,

"Together as one."

The female part was next. Melody peered at the sheet music, cleared her throat, then sang:

"To you I pledge my heart, my life,

"Man and wife,

"Forever as one."

Every note was perfectly pitched.

Luke paused to tease her. "See, was that so painful?"

"Excruciating." Her azure eyes twinkled.

With a chuckle, he proceeded through the song. When they reached the chorus, Melody sang descant and the blended harmony touched Luke's soul. He thought he could listen to Melody sing all day long. Even sight-reading her voice rang out like a professional's. The only unpleasant notes came from Luke's poor piano playing.

After they sang the last word, Luke looked over at her.

"What do you think?"

"It's. . ." She faltered and ran her fingertips over the piano's ivory keys. "It's really a lovely piece, *I suppose.*"

He laughed and gave her a playful nudge with his elbow. "So what's the verdict? Do we sing the duet?"

He held his breath.

She hesitated but then nodded. "Yeah, we'll sing the duet."

Luke rejoiced, sensing this was no small victory!

❧

It was the middle of June, and Darla and Max's wedding day had arrived. Melody dressed with the bride and the other bridesmaids in the spacious library of the church. Darla's white dress was an exquisite creation of pearls and lace, and the bridesmaids' tea-length gowns were a lovely magenta.

Brushing out her hair, Melody calmed her nerves by silently reciting one of her favorite Bible passages from Jeremiah: *"For I know the plans I have for you. . .plans to prosper you and not to harm you, plans to give you hope and a future."*

God had a plan for her life. She could trust Him—even when she couldn't trust herself and her own wayward emotions.

Melody had rehearsed the duet with Luke enough times now that it no longer felt agonizingly uncomfortable. She made up her mind not to think about him standing next to her, singing words of love. Instead, she focused on the Lord Jesus and glorifying Him, praying the duet would be a blessing to Darla and Max.

However, last night at the dress rehearsal her determination almost crumbled. As they sang the refrain about undying love, Luke placed his hand on the small of her back. The inflection in his voice was unmistakable, and Melody had felt her knees weaken. She almost believed he was singing to her.

But, of course, he wasn't. Luke obviously gave the song his all because of his friendship with Max. Melody longed to do the same out of her love for Darla, and now she fought to get her derailed thoughts back on track before she had to sing with Luke again.

"For I know the plans I have for you. . .plans to prosper you and not to harm you, plans to give you hope and a future."

"You can do this," she murmured to her reflection. "With God all things are possible."

Once the bridal party was ready, the ladies gathered in the foyer of the church. The choir director, Ken Bartlet, sat at the organ. He had agreed to accompany Melody and Luke on the piano when it came time for their duet. The number would be memorable; Mel had no doubt.

The wedding procession began. Melody walked up the aisle with Max's younger brother then took her place in line at the altar. Pastor Dan Rebholtz, who knew the couple well, gave them a short challenge and read from the scriptures. Next vows were said and rings exchanged. Mel felt herself grow teary-eyed as Darla and Max promised to love, honor, and cherish. Finally the pastor asked all heads to bow as he prayed for the newly married couple.

This was Melody's cue. Just as they rehearsed last evening, she silently stepped down from the altar and walked to the far aisle where Luke already waited, poised and ready to sing. Melody thought he looked terrific in his black tux, and she gave him a smile as she moved in beside him.

But that's when she noticed it. Only one microphone. Yesterday there were two!

She turned to Luke with wide eyes, and he realized the problem. He calmly adjusted the mike in its stand to accommodate the both of them, which would probably work fine, Mel decided, since her voice carried adequately without amplification. However, that was the least of her concerns. One shared microphone meant she'd have to stand closer to Luke.

Lord, I think those plans You have for me just ran amok.

Luke took a half step back and indicated that she should

scoot in closer to the mike. He slipped his right arm around her waist in what seemed a polite gesture, as it eliminated the awkwardness of their close proximity. Mel had to admit, it was better this way than battling elbows. Unfortunately for her, she suddenly feared she might melt into one giant heap of magenta chiffon.

The choir director took his seat at the piano and began to play. Mel prayed her voice wouldn't betray her.

Think of Jesus. You're singing for His glory.

Luke started off the duet; Melody joined in at the appropriate time. They reached all the right notes and not a beat was missed. As they sang, the bride and groom lit the unity candle, symbolizing their oneness in marriage.

Several minutes later, the song ended, and Melody made her way back up to the altar and took her place among the rest of the bridesmaids.

Triumph soared within Melody. She felt like cheering. She'd done it! She sang in public. God hadn't taken away her gift; it had merely been in hibernation.

fifteen

Do you two sing at weddings often?"

Melody grinned and looked over at Luke. People had been asking them that question all afternoon. Now as they stood in the elegant lobby of the hotel before dinner, several more guests approached them.

"Actually, this is our first wedding," Luke replied to the elderly woman standing in front of him.

"Well, I'd say you both are on the brink of a new career. That song was just beautiful. Why, I never heard voices blend so exceptionally well!"

"Thank you," Melody said, feeling her cheeks warming with embarrassment.

She and Luke smiled at each other.

The white-haired woman took a step with her walker.

"Would you like some assistance getting seated in the banquet hall?" Luke asked her.

Melody grinned, thinking Luke was about as gallant as they came.

"Oh, no, young man, I'll be fine. My great-niece is waiting for me near the door. See her? There she is!"

A girl about twelve years old waved, and the older woman shuffled off in her direction.

Then Bonnie hailed them. "Hey, you guys!"

Melody glanced to her right in time to see her sister's approach. Scott trailed a few steps behind her. He seemed distracted, and Mel wondered if he felt bored.

"You sounded great at the ceremony," Bonnie gushed, smiling first at Luke, then at Melody. Next she hooked her arm around Scott's elbow and pulled him right up beside her. "We want you to sing at our wedding. Will you?"

Mel tensed. The duet might have gone well today by God's grace, but she wasn't sure she wanted to chance it again in a year. What if Luke and Alicia were engaged by then? How would it feel to sing with Luke under those circumstances?

She sent him a tentative glance.

"I'm willing," he said with a shrug and a chuckle. He turned his honey-colored gaze on Melody. "What do you think?"

"Um. . ." Lost in his stare, she almost forgot the question. "I—I don't know. . ."

"Plenty of time to think about it," Luke said. "Besides, by the time Bonnie and Scott get married, you'll be an old pro, Melody."

She snapped to reality. "Oh, yeah? How's that?"

"You'll have a year of singing with the church choir under your belt."

"You're joining choir again, Mel?" Bonnie's blue eyes widened with surprise. "Dad'll be happy to hear that."

"I'm *thinking* about it." Melody tossed a look of mock annoyance at Luke.

He laughed.

Bonnie grinned and gazed around the lobby. "This is a nice place, and I hear the Terrace Room, where we'll have dinner, is gorgeous."

"Oh, it is. There are two magnificent crystal chandeliers hanging from the sculptured ceiling and the ivory wallpaper is trimmed with gold velvet. I helped decorate last night. We placed vases filled with white roses in the center of each table. They add just the right touch." Mel tipped her head and regarded her sister. "Are you thinking of having your reception here, too?"

"Maybe. But what I really want is to rent is the Mitchell Park Pavilion."

"At The Domes?" Mel clenched her jaw and willed away her envy. The Mitchell Park Horticultural Conservatory Domes, often called The Domes, was where she always dreamed about holding her wedding reception. The Domes were three glass beehive-shaped buildings that encompassed a colorful, eye-pleasing array of gardens, from desert blooms to jungle blossoms. Melody could well imagine her reception there and all her wedding pictures taken in the facility also.

Had Bonnie read her personal diary or something? Everything Melody dreamed of her younger sister obtained for herself.

But then Melody cast a glance at Luke and decided she didn't care. If Luke fell in love with her and proposed, she'd marry him *anywhere*, and she wouldn't mind where they held the wedding reception.

The very idea took her breath away.

"Well, I suppose we'd better get seated," Bonnie said. She looked over her shoulder for Scott. He'd strolled off and now stood examining the framed artwork. "Come on, honey."

Melody rolled her eyes at the endearment, then happened to catch Scott cast a long, appreciative gaze at a shapely woman in a low-cut gown striding past him. Mel sucked in a breath and told herself she shouldn't be surprised. She never thought Scott had really changed all that much from their college days.

But did she dare tell that to Bonnie?

Scott noticed her watching him, and Mel snapped her gaze away. He fortunately said nothing as he stepped in beside Bonnie. She took his hand before they proceeded toward the banquet room.

What a hypocrite.

Mel turned to Luke. "Did you see that?"

Luke arched his dark brown brows. "Scott's roving eye?" He nodded. "I've seen it a number of times."

Melody felt her jaw drop. "Why didn't you say something?

We have to warn Bonnie."

Luke took her hand and tucked it around his elbow. "And how many times have you sounded the alarm already, Princess Melody?"

Hearing his nickname for her, a grin pulled at her mouth. "All right. Point taken." Mel knew she'd only be the *bad guy* in this situation once more. "You're right. We'll just have to pray God shows her and my parents the truth somehow."

Luke nodded in agreement as they walked across the plush gold and maroon carpet and entered the Terrace Room. Melody disengaged her hand and took a step toward the head table. Her place was with the bridal party.

He tipped his head slightly. "See you later."

She smiled at the promise before heading for the other side of the room. The bridesmaids sat on one side and the groomsmen on the other.

"Did you hear the sad news?" Wendy Tomlinson asked as Mel sat down and arranged the frilly skirt of her gown.

"Alicia and Jeremy broke up. Happened last night."

"You're kidding?" Melody tried to hide her sudden trepidation. Then guilt set in. She should feel badly for Alicia instead of worrying about herself. But try as she might to suppress them, those niggling doubts spilled into her consciousness. If Alicia Sims broke up with her boyfriend, it meant she was *available*.

"Yeah, Alicia's mom was just diagnosed with breast cancer," Wendy said, "and Jeremy is a rather high-maintenance guy. He wants Alicia's undivided attention, and right now she can't give that to him because her mother's ill."

"Understandable." Mel took a sip from the goblet of ice water in front of her. She hoped to swallow down her flustered feelings. On one hand, she was sad to hear about Mrs. Sims, but on the other, she felt scared of losing Luke.

It was then Melody realized that, in spite of her best efforts, she'd fallen in love with her next-door neighbor.

"Oh, look," Wendy said, leaning over closer to Mel. "Alicia is sitting next to Luke."

Melody forced herself to glance out over the banquet room. Unmistakable dread grew inside of her when she spotted him at one of the round, white linen-covered tables, conversing with the lovely blond whose thick, straight hair hung to her shoulders in perfection. Melody then noticed Alicia's striking red- and silver-trimmed dress that hugged her slim frame.

Lord, help me. I don't want to live with this jealousy and envy.

"That'll be perfect," Wendy prattled on. She gave her French twist a pat as if to be sure every bobby pin was still in place. "Luke took care of both his parents before they died, so he'll know how to encourage Alicia."

Mel supposed that much was true. She recalled the in-depth discussion she and Luke had about his parents, their illnesses, and deaths. As Luke had unburdened his heart that evening as they sat on his back deck with Lexi, Melody got the impression it was a therapeutic event for him. Later Luke said he hadn't ever confided in anyone like he did Melody.

"Alicia, that poor thing. She's really going through it."

And Luke is certainly in the habit of rescuing damsels in distress, Melody thought as her heart took a plunge.

All she had to do was think back on the last couple of months and all the times he'd shown up at the precise moment she needed him most. How foolish she'd been to take him for granted all these years.

Was it too late now to change things?

❧

Melody wrestled with her emotions as the formal dinner progressed—tossed salad, followed by the most incredible veal cordon bleu that Melody ever tasted. By the time slices of wedding cake were served, she'd asked God to help her cast aside all doubts, insecurities, and fears. Tonight's celebration was in honor of Max and Darla's union, after all. It wasn't about Melody Cartwright.

As she prayed through the tumult, a sense of calm settled over her, and Mel decided to just be herself and have fun. When the meal was over, she milled about the Terrace Room, talking and laughing with her friends. From time to time her gaze met Luke's, and he'd send her a smile from across the way.

Then the slide show began. One of Max's friends was a computer whiz and put together the most amazing pictures that spanned the newlyweds' lives thus far. First babies, next toddlers, through elementary school and high school. Melody laughed when she glimpsed herself in a few snapshots. She'd been a gangly kid, somewhat of a tomboy who loved animals and climbed trees. But she also had a feminine side of her that enjoyed playing house and mothering her baby dolls.

Mel had to chuckle again when a photo flashed up on the screen of all the guys playing basketball. Mel guessed they were about seventeen, and what a goofy-looking bunch! Max had always been the tallest, so he stood in the back row. Luke was beside him, thin as a reed, wearing those midnineties teardrop glasses that took up most of his face.

"Praise God we don't stay teenagers forever."

Melody heard Luke's voice right behind her. "Amen!" she agreed with another laugh.

When the viewing ended, Mel was called away for another set of pictures with Darla and Max and the entire bridal party. Later she wandered out onto the veranda and sat down next to Jamie Becker on a cushioned settee. Her toes felt pinched in the strappy high heels she'd worn all day. In two discreet moves, she kicked them off and folded her legs under her skirt.

A small circle of six friends surrounded her in padded chairs. Tim, Military Mike, Bob, and Keith were at their obnoxious worst. They teased each other about the earlier slide show and laughed as they remembered humorous things about each other. Mel found them amusing and egged them on, tossing in a few of her own memories.

"And then, of course, there was the time that Bob was practicing before a baseball game," she said, "and he accidentally threw the bat through the sanctuary's stained glass window."

Everyone hooted, although it hadn't been funny when it occurred.

"Must you encourage them?" Jamie asked with a sidelong glance at Melody.

Mel didn't see any harm in the banter but gulped back the retort on her tongue. Jamie had attended a different high school, and Melody sometimes wondered if she felt left out.

But then, including her in their walk down memory lane, Keith began teasing Jamie about the time the youth group went to Chicago at Christmastime and she got lost in an upscale department store. The youth pastor's wife found her in the lingerie department.

"I wasn't *shopping* there," Jamie said, but everyone else was laughing too loudly to hear her defense. Finally she stood and stomped off.

"Now you did it." Mel flicked her gaze upward.

"Aw, she'll forgive us," Mike said, straightening the jacket of his formal military blues.

"Yeah, she always does," Bob added, clasping his beefy hands.

Keith spouted off a goofy comeback and the rowdy laughter started all over again. Melody found herself giggling just because they were chuckling so hard.

"This seat taken?"

Mel glanced up and saw Luke standing beside the settee. She managed a straight face long enough to tell him the spot was vacant.

Luke filled it. But Melody soon realized he took up a lot more space than Jamie's skinny frame. They knocked elbows as Luke made himself comfortable, and Mel thought he still looked dapper in spite of the fact he'd shed his jacket. The night air was balmy, and she felt warm in her sleeveless dress so she imagined how hot and uncomfortable a black wool tuxedo jacket would feel.

"Okay, boys, settle down," Bob said. "Luke's here so we have to act sophisticated." He had a slight lisp and perspiration trickled down the side of his pudgy face. "Luke thinks we're professionals like him, so we have to uphold our image."

"Yeah, whatever, you guys." Luke grinned and stretched his arm out across the back of the settee. He crossed his legs, the calf of his left resting on the knee of his right. "I grew up with all of you, remember? I know who you *really* are."

More chuckles and wise remarks emanated from the group, and Wendy piped up, giving the boys something else to howl at.

At this point, however, Mel wasn't paying any attention to the verbal volleying. Her thoughts were consumed with how pleasurable it felt to sit next to Luke this way. She had to fight the urge to rest her head on his shoulder.

Then he leaned over and whispered close to her ear, and it suddenly felt much warmer on the long, wide cement porch. "Darla's cousin asked if we'd sing at her wedding in the fall. She said she'll pay us."

She turned and regarded him, thinking his honey-brown eyes appeared like polished topaz under the soft glow of the outdoor lights.

"What do you think?" she hedged.

Luke shrugged and pursed his lips in momentary thought. "My schedule is pretty much my own so I can plan around showings if I know about something in advance. How about you? How do you feel about singing at another ceremony—that's not your sister's?"

"I guess." She shrugged. "I wouldn't mind, but. . ." She considered Alicia and tried to imagine where Luke's relationship would be with her by then, assuming all went according to his hopes and plans.

And then it occurred to Mel that her present close proximity to Luke wasn't going to help him capture Alicia's affections. Didn't he realize that? Sure, they'd known each other forever, but had they become such good friends that Luke felt, perhaps, too comfortable around Melody now?

"Give the matter some prayer time," Luke said with a gentle smile that quickened her pulse. "We can let her know at a later date."

Mel bobbed out a silent reply.

"You two make such a cute couple," Wendy said.

Melody caught the enthusiastic spark in her girlfriend's eyes.

"Better make sure you catch the bridal bouquet, Mel," Bob told her with a conspiratorial wink. "That'll mean you're getting married next."

"Hold her back, Luke," Mike said. His indigo eyes widened as he feigned an alarmed expression. "Hold her back, or you're a marked man."

Melody laughed off the implications. She expected Luke to refute the misunderstanding anytime now, although she refrained giving their friends any explanation. The deepest, most vulnerable part of her wished she and Luke were a "cute couple." However, the fact was they weren't even dating!

But to Melody's absolute astonishment, Luke chuckled and said nothing to the contrary.

sixteen

I have to set Luke straight, Mel decided on the drive back home once the reception ended. She'd stayed well past midnight to help collect personal items and tidy up the banquet hall with the other bridesmaids. Meanwhile, Darla and Max left to spend their first night together at a hotel near the airport. Mel glanced at the digital clock on her dashboard that read 2:00 and realized in just a matter of hours, her dear friends would be on their way to Hawaii for their honeymoon.

Melody hoped she'd have the opportunity to marry and experience a romantic honeymoon. Somewhere deep within her being she felt a longing to be loved, honored, and cherished—and to say "I do."

But it didn't appear her dreams would come true anytime soon.

Now what to do about Luke. . .

Melody pulled in next to Bonnie's compact SRT and parked beneath the carport. She collected her purse and duffel bag containing her bridesmaid's dress, shoes, stockings, and the cosmetics she'd used before the wedding. Once everyone had left the reception, Melody had changed back into her blue jeans and a T-shirt to help with the cleanup.

She made her way to the house and couldn't help casting a glance at Luke's place. All lights were off and she thought of Lexi, her "baby." Mel couldn't wait to play with her again, and she was grateful to Tom and Emily Wheeler who'd agreed to puppy-sit so Luke could enjoy the reception tonight.

Somehow I have to tell him that our friendship crossed the boundaries, at least where I'm concerned. And what about our friends? They all think we're the next Darla and Max.

Melody unlocked the side door and walked in. *Luke is never going to get Alicia the way he's going!*

More than once tonight, Melody entertained ideas of how she might steal Luke's heart. After all, it wasn't as though Alicia would find out what she did and feel hurt. Alicia had no clue of Luke's interest. But Melody recalled Luke saying he wanted God to orchestrate the match between him and the woman with whom he'd spend the rest of his life. If Mel set out to manipulate the situation, she sensed that she would end up with another broken heart and she didn't think she could bear two in the same lifetime.

But could she suffer through losing Luke's friendship?

≈

The next morning at church Melody had every intention of being cordial to Luke but aloof at the same time. She planned to discuss the particulars of their relationship with him as soon as time permitted. She wanted to explain her feelings—if she could, by God's grace, articulate them. But as she stood in the doorway of the sanctuary, looking around for a place to sit, her gaze immediately connected with Luke's. It was almost as if no one else existed.

He smiled and pointed to the blue padded chair beside him, and Melody nodded. Before she knew it, she'd seated herself next to him.

"Good morning."

"Morning." Melody felt the fingers of chagrin working their way up her neck and into her cheeks. She'd done exactly what she promised herself she wouldn't do. But somehow she couldn't seem to help it. "How come you're not in choir?"

He leaned into her shoulder. "Tom and Em stayed over-night, so I missed practice to have breakfast with them."

"That's nice—I mean, not that you missed practice, but that you ate breakfast with the Wheelers." Mel could have smacked herself. Now she'd lost her ability to communicate altogether.

"I know what you meant." Luke chuckled and straightened in his chair.

She gave him an appreciative stare. As always, he was impeccably dressed. He wore a black suit, French-blue shirt, and a printed tie that complemented the ensemble.

"They say hello."

"What? Who?" Mel forced her attention back to the conversation.

"Tom and Em."

"Oh, of course."

She didn't have to see her reflection to know her face flushed crimson, but the choir's opening number saved her from further humiliation.

After a soul-stirring rendition of "Be Thou My Vision," the congregation was asked to stand and sing. Minutes later, the Wisbreck family played their woodwind instruments while the offering plates were passed.

Then Pastor Miller took the pulpit. Tall, blond, and in his seventies, he had a smooth-as-whipped-vanilla-pudding voice, and he resembled a gentle father figure to those under thirty. The older members of the church considered him a faithful friend and man of God. His message this morning caused Melody's spirit to take flight and helped her put things back into their proper perspective.

"Loneliness," the pastor said as he adjusted his bifocals, "overtakes us only when our joy is dependent on someone or something else."

He went on to emphasize that a person can feel lonely even with crowds of people surrounding him. A woman might feel lonely, in spite of the fact she's married. Same with a husband.

"Therefore, the answer to loneliness is the love of Christ. He has to fill that hole in your being before another person can."

Melody scribed notes in her wire-bound journal as the pastor spoke.

"Jesus is the Friend who will never leave or disappoint us. Just look at this promise recorded in the book of Isaiah. 'Then will you call, and the Lord will answer; you will cry for help, and he will say: Here I am. . .'"

Love for her Savior swelled in Mel's heart as those words echoed in her mind. *"Here I am. . ."*

Thank You for this reminder, Lord. I'll never be lonely with You in my heart—even if I'm always a bridesmaid.

She expelled a disappointed sigh, not intended for anyone's ears but God's. However, Luke somehow heard it.

"You okay?" he whispered.

"Yeah," Melody whispered back. "Just fine."

However, that "hole in her being," as Pastor termed it, felt like it was gaping.

Lord, You're going to have to help me. I love Luke. She closed her eyes. Had she set herself up for yet another failed relationship? The fiasco with Scott had been more than she thought she could bear.

After the service, Melody stood, collected her purse and Bible. Luke tucked his large, black, leather-bound copy of God's Word under his arm, and they walked out of the sanctuary together.

"Are you busy this afternoon?" Melody still wanted to talk.

"Yeah, I have to show a house. You know I try not to schedule these things on the Lord's Day, but—"

"Yeah, I know." She'd learned months ago that a free Sunday in the real estate business was a rarity.

Luke glanced at his wristwatch. "I'm going to be late. Would you mind letting Lexi out?"

"Not at all."

"Great. Thanks." He gave her a grateful grin. "I'll see you when I get home."

"Sure."

She watched him exit the front doors of the building and jog through the parking lot.

And then it dawned on her that their parting conversation just now sounded far too familiar for "just friends." Passersby who didn't know better would likely think she and Luke were married. *I'll see you when I get home.*

Melody made a mental note, adding this latest concern to her list of discussion topics.

&

As it happened, Mel never did get her chance to speak with Luke on Sunday. Business kept him at the office until the evening worship service. Melody met him at church and while they sat together again, there wasn't any time for a meaningful conversation. Afterward, Luke apologized before dashing back to the office. He had to catch up on several issues, so Melody returned to his place and took care of Lexi. But by ten o'clock, she felt exhausted and couldn't wait for Luke another minute. She traipsed home, changed into her pajamas, and crawled into bed.

And then Monday morning arrived.

Melody stayed busy at the dental office, checking in patients, updating their accounts, and billing various insurance companies for last month's visits, but she managed to make it to Luke's at lunchtime. She let the puppy outside and played with her for a while before setting Lexi back into the crate. She thought it was odd that Luke didn't show up, since he usually did. Mel had been half hoping he'd bring her some lunch, but since that wasn't the case, she purchased a cheeseburger and chocolate shake on the way to work.

That evening, it was much the same scenario. Mel stopped at Luke's house around five, let Lexi out, and played with her in the backyard before crating her again. Mel ate supper at home, which meant enduring Scott's shenanigans. He always managed to do something obnoxious and tonight was no exception. When the meal was finished, Melody carried a stack of plates into the kitchen. Scott was on his way back from the bathroom and he purposely walked into her as they passed. The load in her arms teetered, and Melody thought for sure her mother's treasured dinnerware was about to crash to the floor. Fortunately, Mel regained her balance—and without any help from Scott. Then, as if bumping into her wasn't enough to fuel her agitation, he followed up his dubious act, by saying, "Hey, Mellow, watch where you're going, will ya?"

Mom, Dad, and Bonnie all turned in their seats at the dining room table to see what was going on and, of course, Scott appeared the innocent one, while Mel looked like her sister's traitor.

She fumed as she scrubbed the roasting pan with more vigor than necessary, and she prayed her parents and Bonnie wouldn't make a big deal out of the incident.

With the kitchen cleaned, Mel decided to escape to Luke's place. *Wait until he hears about Scott's latest antics.* She hoped he'd arrived home by now so she could tell him.

The night air felt humid and uncomfortable as Mel made her way next door. It was impossible to see into Luke's garage, so she couldn't tell if his SUV was parked or not.

She reached his side door, unlocked it, and let herself in. When she reached the kitchen, Lexi pranced in from the living room to greet her, so Mel knew Luke was home.

"Luke?" She bent to give the puppy several affectionate strokes before heading through the dining area. "Hey, Luke, you're not going to believe what happened—"

Melody halted in midsentence, seeing Alicia Sims and Pastor Miller seated comfortably the living room. Luke sat in an armchair and twisted around to smile a greeting at her.

Mel returned the gesture. "Sorry, I didn't know you had company."

"That's okay. Come on in and join us."

She stepped forward, about to take Luke up on his offer, but then out of the corner of her eye, Mel spied Pastor Miller's colorfully bound eight-inch by twelve-inch booklet that he'd put together on the topic of courtship. She'd seen it enough times; the homemade publication was available for free at church. It sat front and center at the welcome booth, and Melody even owned a copy.

Her heart lurched. "Um—I just remembered I have to do something." She backtracked. "Sorry to have interrupted."

"You're not interrupting," Alicia said with a pleasant smile. "Come sit down."

Mel shook her head. She wasn't about to sit in on the planning stages of Luke and Alicia's courtship. She'd likely lose her supper. "I have to go."

She fought to keep her voice light and friendly. She'd promised the Lord, after all. She'd never be lonely with Jesus in her heart. "But it's good to see you both again." She sent Pastor her best grin before spinning on her heel and striding toward the door. She tried not to run.

On the way out, she glanced at her house and realized her choices were next to nil. She could hole up in her stuffy room or listen to Bonnie and Mom make wedding plans. It seemed Cupid's arrows were flying everywhere and Melody felt caught in the crossfire.

Keys in hand, she decided on a drive. She strode to her Cavalier, climbed in, and started the engine. She took a deep breath and prayed for calm as she backed out of the carport.

It was only after she'd driven several blocks that she realized she'd left her purse and cell phone at home. She blew out a breath, pondered the matter, and then decided it wouldn't matter. She wasn't planning to stay out for long.

seventeen

Luke sat back in the black leather executive's chair and put his feet up on the corner of his cherry-finished desk. He stared at the photograph of himself and Melody and his heart twisted. The photo had been taken at a wedding they attended this last spring. His buddy at work had given him the picture, so Luke framed it and kept it next to his computer up here in his home office. The snapshot served as a reminder to pray for his future with Mellie, although things didn't look so great at the moment.

Monday night she broke her promise to him and took off in that sassy yellow coupe of hers. He tried to reach her on her mobile phone, but she didn't answer his call. He felt so worried about her that he ended up telling Pastor Miller and Alicia Sims everything. Neither was surprised. His feelings for Melody were quite obvious—and to everyone except Melody.

After he shared his heart, the three of them asked God to protect Melody and they prayed for His perfect will to be done. Luke had to admit the time of prayer with Pastor and Alicia stilled the tumult inside of him. What's more, he sensed it helped Alicia, too. She was full of questions about her mother's upcoming surgery and chemotherapy. She also loved Jeremy, and it appeared the two would get back together soon.

At the wedding reception this past Saturday Alicia had asked Luke if she could stop by and continue their dinner discussion about her mother's illness. Luke agreed and invited Pastor over for extra advice and spiritual support. It would have been an added blessing had Melody joined them that night, but instead she acted like they all had the plague.

Lord, what is it with this woman?

Luke lifted the picture and cradled its silver frame in his hands. He stared at Melody's smiling face and thought over the events that occurred yesterday. Luke had a hunch she went out of her way to avoid him.

Well, she wasn't going to get away with that nonsense today. Luke set down the picture and glanced at his wristwatch. He had an appointment at two thirty, but he planned to be home when Melody came over after work to let Lexi outside.

❧

The sun shone down, bright and hot, from a cloudless blue sky as Melody parked her car. She was glad the carport provided her vehicle with some shade. The temperature soared into the nineties, and the air was thick and muggy so after entering the house and climbing the stairs to her bedroom, she changed out of her scrubs into a lightweight cotton dress that she could wear to church this evening.

She opened the porch door and eyed Luke's house, deciding he wasn't home which meant the puppy needed attention. But as she made her way next door, she hoped it was one of those days where Luke had appointments all the way up until the time the midweek worship service began. Melody just wanted to stay out of his way for now. Once the Lord healed her heart, she'd be able to feel happy for him and Alicia.

Mel unlocked the side door and let herself into Luke's house. He hadn't turned on his air conditioning since the weather had been cooler yesterday and last night. But now his home was beginning to heat up.

Mel opened the crate and the puppy, now four months old, bounded out with her tail wagging. Mel stroked her soft fur. "How's my baby this afternoon?"

As if in reply, Lexi bolted for the living room.

"Hey, come back here!"

The rambunctious dog ran through the house, circling the

kitchen, dining room, and living room. Melody laughed as she watched the puppy doing laps.

Picking up Lexi's leash, Mel decided it was time to go outside. She whistled for the puppy, who continued tearing through the house.

Then Lexi took off up the steps.

Melody groaned and started after her. In all the months she'd been hanging out at Luke's place, Mel never had a cause to go upstairs; however, she knew from him telling her about all the remodeling he had done that four bedrooms and Luke's office were up there.

Along with one very hyper puppy running to and fro, up and down the hallway.

"Lexi, come."

Mel tried to chase her down, but it was no use. The dog ran from one room to the next. However, it did give Melody a chance to check out the second floor of Luke's home.

At one end of the hallway was a guest room with beige carpeting and multicolored quilt covering the full-size mattress. Across the hall was obviously Luke's weight room, as a large home gym contraption loomed in the center of the hardwood floor. Melody imagined him working out and felt oddly impressed.

In the middle of the hallway was a large bathroom. It had white ceramic tile on the floor and a newer-looking sink, vanity, and bathtub. Through the glass shower doors, she noticed the molded plastic tub surround—and the general neatness of the blue and white room. Luke might be a bachelor who hated to grocery shop, but he certainly was no slob.

At the other end of the tan carpeted hall were Luke's bedroom and his office. Melody didn't enter his room, feeling as though she'd be trespassing on sacred ground if she did, although she allowed herself a quick peek. Masculine cherry furniture occupied the wall space and his bed was neatly made, covered with a black, white, and teal patterned spread.

Lexi suddenly ran past her and scooped up one of Luke's leather shoes from off the floor.

"Hey, put that down!" Melody tried to sound firm, but she couldn't contain her giggles. She made a grab for Lexi's collar, but the dog bolted past her. Then she paused at the top of the stairs and dropped the shoe. It tumbled down with several decisive thuds. Next, the pooch scampered into Luke's office.

"Lexi, no!"

Melody grimaced when she heard something hit the floor. She followed the puppy into the office and found the plastic trash bin on its side. Paper had spilled out onto the floor. The puppy lifted a crumpled wad with her jaws and took off again.

Ooooh, that dog is going to get it.

Melody righted the plastic wastebasket and picked up the discarded paper. The puppy stood at the doorway, wagging her tail and panting.

"Don't you laugh at me, you naughty thing."

Lexi scurried off again.

Melody began to feel irritated. It was way too hot for a game of chase. Her hands on her hips, she listened for the dog, hoping Lexi would come back if she didn't run after her this time.

At that very moment, Mel blinked and her line of vision came into focus. She saw a silver framed photograph perched beside Luke's computer. *That's us!*

She crossed the room and lifted the sturdy frame. She examined the picture and realized it was taken at the wedding she'd attended with Luke a couple of months ago.

"Now why would he have something like. . ."

Before she finished her spoken thought, the answer hit her like a two-ton brick. Her mind rewound time, then played back incident after incident.

She recalled their tender encounters, like the many times

he'd taken her hand in his—a gesture of mere kindness, or so Mel had led herself to believe. They were just friends, right? But what about those instances when he placed his arm around her waist or stretched it across the back of the love seat on which they sat?

He faithfully phoned her every day, asking if she had plans for the evening. She seldom did, so Luke always came up with an appealing idea. A walk by the lakefront. A Brewers baseball game at Miller Park. Sitting out on his back deck and talking. He treated her to lunch and took her out to dinner at upscale restaurants, always refusing Melody's offers to pay. Didn't friends take turns picking up the tab? Luke wouldn't hear of it. And if she even hinted at a need, he was there to meet it.

Luke wasn't just a friend, although he certainly had become the best friend she'd ever had. No, he had been *pursuing her*.

And all the while she had been falling in love with him.

Oh, duh!

By now, Lexi had returned and sat beside Mel, licking her ankle. Mel glanced down at the puppy. "Stop that!"

Mel wiped the slobber off her leg with one hand and returned the framed snapshot to its place on Luke's desk with the other. Then she clapped the leash onto Lexi's collar.

"Well, I guess I know who Mystery Girl is," she told the mischievous but lovable mutt. "It's me."

Even as she spoke the words, a sense of disbelief engulfed her. But it had to be—and suddenly everything fell into place like pieces of a jigsaw puzzle. The total picture filled Melody with awe and happiness.

The sound of a door closing downstairs jolted her back to reality. Luke was home and it wouldn't be cool if he found her in his office.

Her fist around the leash, Mel led the dog to the stairway. She got about halfway down when Luke appeared. He wore tan trousers and a navy blue, short-sleeved polo shirt and as he peered up the stairwell at her, he finger-combed his nut-brown hair off his forehead.

"Hi."

"Hi." Melody grinned, watching him retrieve his shoe off the step.

He gave her a curious look.

"Your dog."

"Ah. . ." He glanced at the black wingtip.

Melody descended a couple more steps. "She's a bundle of energy this afternoon."

Lexi wagged her tail and chomped at the tassel on the top of the shoe. Luke raised his hand, and she jumped for it. "Hey, this isn't yours."

Mel smiled and let go of the leash. Freed once more, Lexi forgot the shoe and pranced into the kitchen. She then slurped noisily from her water dish.

"She hasn't been outside yet," Mel explained. "She was running around your house like maniac."

A look of amusement wafted across his features as he tossed his shoe up the stairs. Next he removed his dark-rimmed glasses and rubbed the perspiration from around the bridge of his nose.

"Say—um—Melody, have I done something to offend you?"

"No, why?" In the next second, she guessed the reason he asked. "Oh. . . You're referring to the last few days."

"Yes, I am." Luke put his glasses back on, leaned against the corner of the stairwell, and folded his arms. "What's going on? It's like you've been purposely avoiding me."

Melody saw the look of hurt flash in his tawny eyes, and she felt guilty for being the one to inflict it. On the other hand, she didn't want to admit to being such an idiot. After all, she should have known long ago that she was none other than Mystery Girl. The telltale signs had been right in front of her face.

"I—well, I've been struggling with some issues. I needed time to sort everything out in my head." She pushed out a tentative smile. "But the good news is I'm on the right track now."

The explanation sounded lame to Mel's own ears, but it was the best she could come up with—and it wasn't as if she lied.

Luke bobbed out several subtle nods, although the confusion never left his features. "Glad to hear it."

Melody walked down to the next step. She wished she could wipe away Luke's wounded expression. "I'm sorry if I was rude. Please forgive me, all right?"

"Of course. All's forgiven." He searched her face and Mel felt her cheeks warm under his scrutiny. "I just wondered if I'd done something to upset you."

"No, it's not you at all. It's me."

Now he looked concerned. "Want to talk about it?"

Mel shook her head. She sat down on the third step up, deciding she'd feel like an imbecile if she revealed the truth behind her standoffishness the past couple of days. "It really doesn't matter anymore, Luke. Like I said, it's all good. I'm squared away."

Luke put his foot on the first stair and leaned forward, his forearms resting on his thigh. "I hope I didn't do something to lose your confidence."

"No." She wagged her head once more. "No, you've been terrific. I know I can always count on you."

Chagrin inched its way up her neck and face. She wanted to blurt out her misunderstanding about him and Alicia, but the words felt wedged in her throat.

"I'm glad you feel that way. I want you be able to depend on me."

He reached out and tucked several strands of her hair behind one ear and Melody found herself hoping he'd kiss her. He appeared to be considering the idea and the anticipation caused her heart to skip a beat.

But, instead of inching closer, he pulled his chin back and narrowed his gaze. "There is another matter we need to discuss. I'll have you know you broke your promise."

Melody drew her brows together. "What?"

"You promised me you wouldn't take off in your car all alone, but that's exactly what you did on Monday night."

"But, Luke, I didn't have anywhere to go."

Melody told him about how Scott nearly knocked her over after she'd cleared the dinner table.

Luke shook his head in disbelief, and Mel saw the muscle work in his right jaw. She sensed he experienced the same indignation now as she had felt that night.

"Things are making more sense. That's what you wanted to tell me, isn't it?" Luke asked. "That's why you came over Monday night, and when you saw Alicia and Pastor here, you realized we couldn't hold a private conversation."

Melody nodded as relief filled her being. She wouldn't be forced to admit her utter stupidity.

Luke sat one step below her. "Well, I'm sorry I let you down, even if it was unintentional."

"You didn't let me down." She put her hand on his broad, muscular shoulder. "I think that would actually be impossible."

He stared up at her with vulnerability pooling in his honey-colored eyes, a reminder to Melody of his sensitive nature. She loved that quality about him. But just as those very words—"I love you"—were about to slip off the end of her tongue, a crash in the other room dispelled the moment's magic.

A naughty puppy needed to be reckoned with in the kitchen.

eighteen

Melody entered the large bedroom she shared with her sister feeling as if she were part of some incredible fantasy. The birds seemed to sing a little louder. The sunset tonight had looked more vibrant, with silver and violet-red streaked across the horizon. Mel had seen the Master's handiwork as she and Luke left the church tonight—after choir practice—and she could easily imagine those stunning shades as bridesmaids' dresses and in a bridal bouquet.

Her only disappointment came when two of their friends, Marlene and Sarah, asked Luke for a ride home. He obliged them, of course, being the kind and considerate guy he was, and neither woman lived too far out of the way. However, their presences meant Mel couldn't speak with Luke privately, and she'd been eager to tell him how she felt.

But then it occurred to her that God had intervened so she couldn't share her heart with Luke. She had concluded quite some time ago that he was a bit old-fashioned—like the way he always called her "Melody" or "Mellie," but never "Mel." Having realized all that again tonight, she decided she would show him how deeply she cared about him, but allow him to speak words of love to her first.

The only problem was Luke hadn't completely outgrown his bashful nature, especially when it came to expressing his emotions.

Oh, Lord, is this going to take forever?

Mel sighed as she set down her purse on the bureau and turned on the lamp. Patience had never been one of her strong points, and where Luke was inhibited, she was ingenuous.

Maybe that means we'll make a good pair.

Melody kicked off her sandals and strode across the plush peach carpeting.

And that's when she spied Bonnie sitting at the head of her bed with her legs pulled up to her chest.

"Bon-bon, what are you doing?" Mel thought it odd that her sister would sit in the dark all alone. "Are you sick or something?"

In reply, Bonnie lowered her head onto her knees. Her shoulders shook, and Mel knew she was crying.

"Let me guess. You and Scott had your first fight."

Bonnie raised her head and glared at her. "How can you be sarcastic when you can see I'm upset?"

Melody blinked at the comeback. "Sorry. I didn't mean to come off as insensitive."

Bonnie didn't answer, but buried her face once more, and Mel thought about all the times she'd cried out her own heart over Scott. That creep wasn't worth even one single tear, and she wished her younger sister would realize it.

"Look, I'm here if you want to talk," Mel said. "But if you don't, that's fine, too."

Again, no response and Melody didn't push it. She went about her business. After changing her clothes, she booted up her computer and checked her e-mail. She chuckled as she read the joke Luke forwarded to her.

"How can you laugh when my life is falling apart?" Bonnie murmured.

"Sorry, it's this dumb thing Luke sent me."

"You mean you two spend practically every waking hour together, and then he sends you e-mail on top of it?"

Melody shrugged and decided not to add that Luke called her at work at least once a day. "Doesn't Scott send you e-mail?"

"No, he's much too busy."

The note of defensiveness in Bonnie's voice caused Mel to

bristle. "What's he so 'busy' doing? I mean, he's not in school and he only works part-time."

As the last word left her mouth, Mel wished she could suck them all back inside. No doubt she'd just started World War III.

But much to her surprise, Bonnie didn't have a retort, and the silence made Mel feel doubly sorry she'd spouted off.

"Bon-bon, I apologize."

"Forgiven." Bonnie unfolded her limbs and began to change her clothes. "I know you don't like Scott."

Melody clamped her mouth shut, deciding to quit before she really did incite a battle.

"Do you mind if I ask how much Luke knows about your relationship with Scott?"

"Luke knows every ugly detail."

"Does he dislike Scott, too?"

"I don't know." Mel swiveled in her chair to face Bonnie again. "I never asked him point-blank and he never said."

She appeared to think it over, then slipped her nightshirt over her head. "Well, if he doesn't like Scott he hides it pretty well. He was really polite when he showed Scott and me around the Thornton place." Bonnie's voice trembled. "I had high hopes of buying that house. But Scott dragged his feet and someone else's bid was accepted before ours."

"Think of it like this—you were spared a total nightmare."

"Did you see it?"

"Yep." Melody sent Bonnie a teasing grin. "I happen to know the Realtor personally."

"Yeah, I guess you do." Bonnie stretched her slender body. "All our friends are buzzing about the two of you."

Melody tipped her head, digesting the remark. "Yeah, I figured."

"Some of them think you're using Luke to—oh, you know, get over Scott."

"Those who think that aren't *my* friends. And you know

what else? Our career group has some serious issues. Instead of extending mercy to their brothers and sisters in Christ, too many people gossip about them and think the worst."

"I agree."

Mel tried to hide her surprise. She had expected Bonnie to argue the point.

"Jamie's been bad-mouthing Scott."

"Oh?" Mel decided she'd probably agree with Jamie, but she kept her thoughts to herself. Her relationship with Bonnie seemed to be on the mend, and Melody didn't want to do—or say—anything to jeopardize the reconciliation process.

"Yeah, and tonight Scott and I exchanged such terrible words. And it's all because I listened to my friends. I got this crazy idea in my head that Scott doesn't love me anymore."

Bonnie's voice broke, and she began to cry again.

Melody ached for her. She sensed that, in this case, their friends might be right. She stood, crossed the room, and pulled Bonnie into a sisterly embrace. What more could she do? Words only sparked resentment. Bonnie would have to learn the hard way.

Just like she had.

❧

The next morning, Melody was busy at work. When her lunch hour arrived, she grabbed her purse and left the office. She had every intention of driving to Luke's and taking care of the puppy, but as she stepped into the parking lot, someone seized her upper arm in a painful grip. Surprise mingled with irritation rose up inside of her until she turned to face her captor. Then fury set in.

"Scott!" She tried to twist out of his grasp. "What do you think you're doing, sneaking up on me like that?"

"Settle down, all right? I have to talk to you. It's important."

Melody stilled and he released her arm. She rubbed the place where he'd held fast, wondering if he took some diabolical delight in hurting her just now.

"What do you want—and how did you know where I work?"

"Bonnie told me." Dressed in beige cargo shorts and an avocado-green T-shirt with a bold black stripe across the chest, Scott gazed down the sidewalk. Dr. Leonard's dental office was one of six businesses comprised in this small strip mall. "Let's go have lunch at that Chinese place. Then I'll explain."

"I can't. I have to let Lexi out."

He looked back at her. "What I have to say is more important than a dog, I can assure you."

"Lexi is not *just* a dog."

"Whatever. Look, I need to talk to you about Bonnie. But not here." He glanced around. People walked in and out of nearby stores and offices. "Please, I need your help."

Melody recalled her conversation with Bonnie last night about her spat with Scott. No doubt that's what he wanted to discuss. Did he want to know how to make it up to Bonnie?

"Try flowers and candy, Scott. They work every time." Mel grinned then looked at her watch. "I really have to go, or I'll be late getting back. Just tell Bonnie you're sorry. She'll forgive you."

"Mellow, it's not as simple as flowers and candy, and if you don't have lunch with me and hear me out, the consequences will be on your shoulders."

"What?"

"You heard me."

The hard tone of Scott's voice prevented Melody from taking another step. She slowly lifted her gaze to his face. It was met with a stony expression.

Melody mulled over the ultimatum. "I don't want to get in the middle of anything."

"There is no middle."

Mel thought it over some more and finally relented. Something was up, and she knew better than to underestimate Scott's motives.

"Oh, fine, but I have to call Luke and let him know I won't make it home." She reached into her purse and retrieved her mobile phone. "Why don't you get us a table?"

"No, I'll wait." Scott folded his arms.

Mel didn't even try to hide her annoyance as she searched for Luke's office number in her phone bank. When she found it, she pressed the SEND button. To her disappointment, she got his recorded message. Next, she called his cell phone, but, again, reached its voice mail feature. This time she left a message.

"Hi, Luke, it's Mel. I can't get home for lunch, but I'll call you later."

She ended the call, tucked the phone back into her purse, and then grudgingly walked to the restaurant with Scott.

Inside, the place was dimly lit, and the walls were papered in red and gold. Imitation Chinese lanterns hung from the ceiling, and the tables were covered with red plastic cloths. After being escorted to a table for two against the far wall, they sat down. The hostess, a young Asian woman, gave them a smile before handing them menus.

Mel already knew she'd order the buffet. "So what's going on?"

Scott sent her a look of disbelief. "Can we order first?"

"I really don't have time. I'm on my lunch break." Melody tapped her wristwatch to emphasize the point. "Some of us have to work for a living, you know?"

Scott took her teasing to heart and slapped the menu on the table. "Why do you hate me so much?"

"I don't hate you. I just—well, to be perfectly honest, I think you're a jerk. Now tell me what's so important that I had to change my plans."

He narrowed his gaze, but before he could reply, the waitress showed up.

Melody and Scott both ordered the buffet. Then they stood and helped themselves to the various Chinese-American dishes.

Back at the table, Melody bowed her head and thanked God for her meal. She also asked for wisdom and grace to get through this discussion with Scott, although she couldn't imagine what he wanted to tell her.

Scott returned and began eating his lunch. Melody noticed he didn't pray first, but many times she said a swift and silent, *Thank You, Jesus,* before eating, so she reminded herself not to be too hard on Scott—this time.

"Okay, now tell me what's up."

Scott chewed, swallowed, then wiped his mouth with the white paper napkin. "I got accepted to the Mayo Medical School in Minnesota on a full scholarship."

"Congratulations." Melody supposed it was good news. He'd already been accepted to the medical college here in Milwaukee, but now, if he moved to Minnesota, the financial burden of his education would be lifted. "Does Bonnie know?"

"Nope." He popped a piece of deep-fried shrimp into his mouth.

"No?" Mel thought it over then guessed what this was all about. "Oh, listen, I'm sure Bonnie will move wherever she has to in order to get you through medical school. Even if it means leaving her family and friends. Is that what you're worried about?"

Scott shook his head. "Mellow, I can't marry Bonnie."

The remark stole her breath away.

"If I marry her, my financial status will change, and I'll lose my full scholarship."

Melody felt the blood begin to drain from her face. She sensed what was about to come but felt compelled to reason with him. "Bonnie loves you. She'll wait—"

"No." Scott wiped his mouth again. "I decided I'm not ready

to get married."

Mel told herself she shouldn't be surprised. "And you're telling me all this—why? You should be talking to my sister."

Scott didn't look up from his plate. "No, I want you to break the news to Bonnie."

"Me?" Mel gaped at the man. But soon her shock diminished, and her reasoning returned. Scott was planning to pull his old disappearing act once again. "How totally typical of you to shake off your responsibility and leave someone else to clean up the mess. Life is all about you, isn't it? You don't care who you step on and who you hurt as long as you get your way."

He glanced up at her and Mel tried to see some sign of remorse in his eyes, but couldn't find a single trace.

"For as long as I can remember," he said, "I've planned to attend med school. My entire life has revolved around that goal, and I can't let anything or anyone interfere with my achieving it."

"Shouldn't you have thought of that *before* you left a trail of broken hearts in your wake?"

He shrugged and grinned. "I'm an all-American red-blooded male. What can I say?"

"Oh, spare me." She shook her head at the lousy excuse.

But then, as the graveness of the situation set in, all the fight left Mel. Remorse and trepidation took its place.

"Scott, aren't you sad? Don't you love Bonnie? Won't it devastate you to leave her behind?" Melody just couldn't fathom such callousness. "What kind of doctor are you going to be if you're so unfeeling, selfish, and unsympathetic? How can you act like this if you're a Christian?"

"Do you hear yourself? You're asking me about feelings when emotion can't have a place in my life. A person can't get through all the training it takes to become an MD by being warm and fuzzy. It takes backbone and hard work."

"Yeah, both of which you know nothing about." Melody

gathered her purse and stood. She tossed her napkin on top of her barely touched meal. "I'm not saying a word to my sister, Scott. You'll have to tell her yourself."

He caught her wrist as she tried to pass him on the way to the door. "I leave tomorrow."

She pulled out of his grasp. "Good riddance."

The encounter shook Melody more than she cared to admit, and she couldn't flee the restaurant fast enough. She did, however, manage to tell the waitress that "the man sitting over there in the green shirt" would pay the bill. She figured it was the least Scott could do.

Mel jogged up the walk to the dental office. Reaching her desk, she called Luke. Her hands shook with incredulity as she punched in his number. But, just as before, she couldn't reach him.

She opted to leave another message on his cell phone. "Luke, something terrible happened. Scott's breaking up with Bonnie and he wants *me* to tell her. What nerve! Can you believe it?" Mel's voice cracked under all the emotion. "Will you call me at work, Luke? I really need to talk to you."

nineteen

The sun began its evening descent in the western sky when Luke reached the park's baseball field. Earlier today, he'd driven to Chicago for a short seminar with a few business associates, and they hadn't returned to the office until after six o'clock. He had attempted to call Melody several times, but his mobile phone didn't seem to be working. There hadn't been time to use a pay phone, and Luke just figured he'd catch up with her at some point. When he arrived home, Melody and Lexi were nowhere to be found. He presumed Melody had taken the pooch for a walk, but the disappointment he experienced amazed him. His house had never felt emptier. Even so, he did his best to set aside his feelings for the sake of his teammates and changed from his suit and tie into faded blue jeans and a green T-shirt that sported the name "Faith Bible Church." Then he scribbled a note to Melody, grabbed his gear, and set off in his SUV for the baseball diamond.

Luke parked and glanced at the digital clock on his dashboard. He had fifteen minutes to get warmed up and into position. Tonight his team played Creekwood Community Church.

"Luke! Over here!"

His gaze followed the familiar voice until he spotted Keith and his shock of dark, curly hair. Luke jogged toward him and, reaching the bench on which his buddy sat, he deposited his duffel bag against the chain-link fence just behind home plate.

"Glad you made it."

Luke nodded. "Yeah, me, too." Unzipping his bag, he removed his bat and began to stretch. "I spent six hours on the road today—and the seminar in Chicago was only four hours long."

"Worth the drive?"

Luke shrugged. "Sort of, although I'm glad my company picked up the tab."

"I can relate." Keith sat forward and folded his hands over his knees. "So, uh, where's Melody?"

"I haven't talked to her today, but I'm hoping she'll show up to watch the game."

Keith bobbed his head and pursed his lips as if thinking over the remark. "You've got it bad for her, don't you?"

Luke replied with a tight smile. He wasn't about to discuss his feelings for Melody with a third party, even though he'd known Keith since junior high. In fact, he was probably one of Luke's better friends, in spite of the fact that, at times, Keith could be as impetuous as the apostle Peter had been when he cut off the guard's ear.

"Listen, Luke, what if I told you that there's—um—someone else she's seeing that you don't know about?"

"I'd say ignore the rumors and mind your own business." Luke had heard all the talk, and the truth was it hurt Melody more than it bothered him.

"They're not rumors."

Keith stood. He was shorter than Luke by about four inches, but he made up for the lack of height with his broad shoulders and sinewy biceps. He unclamped his cell phone from its holster that he wore on his belt.

"I ate lunch with a friend today at a Chinese place and guess who I happened to see there." He flashed his picture phone at Luke. "Melody—with her sister's fiancé."

Luke took the phone and stared at the picture. It wasn't the best quality, but he could clearly see Melody and Scott Ramsay, seated at table. It appeared they were having an intimate conversation.

He handed the phone back to Keith but said nothing.

"I know it hurts, man, but someone had to set you straight. Mel dated that guy in college, and—"

"I know all about it." Luke held up his hand to forestall further comment, although he had to admit he was curious as to why Melody met Ramsay for lunch. She hadn't said anything about it last night—except she did tell him she'd been struggling with something. Was that "something" Scott Ramsay?

Luke reined in his imagination; he wasn't about to jump to conclusions.

"Look, for all we know, Melody and Scott were discussing a surprise party for Bonnie. Her birthday's next month."

"I don't think so." Keith wore a dire expression. "I couldn't hear exactly what they were saying, but I do know this—Mel was doing her best to talk that guy out of *something*. Then she left in a huff."

"Well, now *that* I can believe." He grinned. Ramsay did aggravate Melody to no end.

Keith, however, wouldn't be assuaged. "Hey, I know love is blind and all that, but, come on. A picture is worth a thousand words."

"Pictures can also be deceiving."

"But—"

Luke cut him off. "I'll talk to Melody."

"And she'll lie to you. What? Do you think she'll admit to secretly seeing her sister's fiancé?"

Luke sighed. "Look, Keith, I know your last girlfriend lied to you, and that was terrible. But you can't judge Melody—or any other woman—by the way Amanda treated you. I know Melody. We both do. She's not a liar."

"Yeah, well, I thought I *knew* Amanda, too." Keith wore a sour expression.

"I know." Luke gave his buddy's shoulder a sympathetic slap. "And I also know the Lord has someone good out there for you. I've been praying for you."

"Thanks." Keith's features lightened, but Luke didn't think his pal was totally convinced of Melody's innocence.

His next words confirmed it.

"I appreciate the prayers, but in the meantime, I've got your back, Luke. We've got the evidence right here." Keith shook his phone at Luke then returned it to its hard plastic holder.

Luke tamped down his irritation. "I don't need evidence. What's more, I'd appreciate it if you'd delete that picture. It's not going to edify anyone, but it could hurt a lot of people if they buy into all the gossip floating around."

Before Keith could utter another syllable, he and Luke were called onto the playing field. The baseball game was about to begin.

ᕬ

Melody read Luke's note and felt relieved when she saw the words "cell phone not working." It explained why she hadn't heard from him all day. Mel had wondered about it since Luke always returned her calls.

But at the rest of his scribed message, she groaned. The last thing she felt like doing was sitting on hard bleachers, getting eaten alive by mosquitoes, and watching an amateur baseball game. She was physically tired and emotionally spent. She'd fretted all afternoon about the bomb that Scott dropped in her lap at lunchtime. Melody just wished she could spill out her troubles to Luke and get everything sorted out in her head. She knew talking to him would calm her troubled spirit. But obviously any discussions had to wait until after his game. She sensed by his note that it was important for her to attend the ball game.

She crated Lexi then ran home to change out of her scrubs and into plaid walking shorts and a red sleeveless shirt. She slipped leather sandals on her feet before scurrying out the door. But when she reached her car, she felt sorry for the dog.

The poor thing had been cooped up all day and to leave her again seemed almost inhumane.

Returning to Luke's place, Melody lifted the leash from its hook in the back hall and opened the crate, setting Lexi free. "Come on, girl. You get to see your very first baseball game."

The puppy replied with a vigorous wag of her long tail.

With Lexi in the backseat of her yellow Cavalier, Mel drove to the county recreational area and found the location where the games were typically held. She'd been here numerous times in the past. Most often she came to gab with her friends and seldom paid attention to the game. As for Luke, she had seldom paid attention to him, either. Until now. Suddenly the church's baseball team held some interest for her.

Mel pulled into the asphalt lot, parked, and climbed out of her car. With Lexi in tow, she strode toward the bleachers. She saw Jamie, Sarah, and Marlene right away and then scanned the dirt diamond and the lawn beyond it. She spotted Luke playing center field. The other team was up to bat.

"What's the score?" she asked, reaching the stands.

"Four to two," Jamie said. She flipped up her sunglasses and set them on top of her head. "We're losing—and we've got an injured player. Keith sprained his ankle."

"Bummer."

Melody looked past her girlfriends to see Keith on the bench with an ice pack covering his foot. But before she could tease him, and express her sympathies afterward, of course, several kids ran over to pet Lexi. Mel was able to get the puppy to sit while the children talked to her and stroked her soft fur.

With Lexi and her admirers occupied for a few moments, Mel glanced out over the field just in time to see Luke catch a fly ball.

"WOO-HOO! Way to go, Luke!"

"Will you cut it out?" Jamie teased, giving Mel a rap on the arm. "All these guys have egos the size of the Great Lakes region. Luke was the only one left who didn't. Now you ruined it—and him."

Melody laughed. At the same time, she caught Luke's gaze and waved. He smiled and waved back. Then out of the corner of her eye, she glimpsed Keith's fierce stare. Melody figured his ankle must be really bothering him to make him so grumpy. He was normally a fun-loving guy.

She sat on the edge of the bleacher next to Jamie and watched a little more of the game.

"Cute dog," Jamie remarked, plucking her sunglasses off her short, salt-and-pepper-colored hair. "Are you puppy-sitting tonight?"

Mel grinned. "Yeah."

"So where are Bonnie and Scott tonight?" Sarah asked, peering around Jamie's narrow shoulders.

"Don't know." Mel tried to sound nonchalant, but her stomach crimped with the reminder of what transpired during lunch today.

"I can't decide if I like Scott or not," Jamie said. "Sometimes he seems charming and very nice and other times I get the feeling he's a creep."

You're right on with the creep business, Melody thought. But she kept silent because when this entire situation blew up, she didn't want to be anywhere near the fallout.

"Hey, Mel, c'mon over here."

At Keith's request, she gazed at him and he motioned her over to the bench.

"I'll hang on to the dog for you," Jamie offered.

Mel handed her the leash.

Sarah leaned forward and her reddish-brown hair fell against her cheek. "Keith probably wants you to run and buy him soda."

"Or a pizza." Jamie rolled her brown eyes.

"Yeah, probably." Mel strode over to where Keith sat with his muscular arms stretched out along the top of the bench.

"What's up?" Mel stood over him, arms akimbo.

"Siddown."

Mel lowered herself onto the bench and watched as Keith extracted his cell phone from where he wore it on his belt. He flipped it open, and Mel wondered if he was making a call while talking to her at the same time. Dialing the pizza parlor? Maybe Jamie was right.

"How was lunch today?" he asked still toying with his phone.

Melody shrugged, wondering what the question was supposed to mean. Was Keith implying he didn't get any lunch and justifying his pizza order?

Then he flashed his phone at her. "I caught you."

"What?" Mel groped to understand what he was saying.

"Look at this picture. I caught you, Miss Two-timer."

Melody gaped at him and ripped the phone out of his hand. She stared at the photo and suddenly her head began to swim. The photo clearly depicted her and Scott at the Chinese restaurant today.

"How'd you get this picture?" Mel's first thought was that this could be Scott's handiwork. She told him she wouldn't cooperate. Was this his way of getting even?

"I was at the restaurant," Keith said.

"I didn't see you there."

"Well, I saw you two with my own eyes, and I took a picture because I knew Luke wouldn't believe it unless I had proof."

Luke. Melody glanced out over the field. He had his back to her, watching another player chase a ball.

She looked back at Keith. "I have every intention of explaining what happened today at lunch to Luke. He'll believe me."

"Mel, you could tell that guy the moon was made of cheese and he'd believe you. That's why God gave Luke a friend like me. To set him straight."

"Set him *straight*?" Mel's heart banged inside her chest so hard that its pulsating beats filled her ears. Luke would believe her—wouldn't he? Or would this be the last straw? Maybe Luke would decide she wasn't worth all the time and trouble.

And she could only imagine what would happen when the gossips, who already believed the worst, saw the picture. They'd have a heyday. What would Luke do then? Believe all of them—or her?

And Bonnie. . . When she saw the picture she'd assume Mel had something to do with Scott breaking off their engagement. Melody's plan to keep her mouth shut had just been obliterated. Now she'd have to say something. But how? What would she say? Bonnie would be devastated. Her parents would never trust her again. She'd have to move out. Find a new church. Everyone would hate her!

Miss Two-timer.

Indescribable anguish filled Melody's being. She closed her eyes against the horror of what she imagined the future would bring. "I can't believe you did this, Keith."

"Me? What about you?" He snatched back his phone.

Mel disregarded his question. "Who have you shown that picture to? Wait. Never mind." She shook her head. "It doesn't matter."

She knew better than anyone that Keith liked to talk. Mel wouldn't put it past him to relay the whole sordid untruth to anyone who'd listen. Even if he didn't have a picture of her and Scott, Keith saw them together. It was too late.

She pushed to her feet, willing her legs to hold her. Her mind whirred as she grappled for a solution. There was none. Her breath came and went in rapid successions as panic threatened to overtake her.

Keith caught her wrist, but Mel twisted out of his grasp. She heard him say something, but the words were indiscernible. Her brain screamed, *What am I going to do? What am I going to do?*

Melody had never felt so helpless in all her life.

Everything seemed surreal as she took the leash from Jamie and then jogged to her car. She felt as though she was in a vacuum and the only voice she heard was her own, crying and pleading for help. *Oh, God, what am I going to do?*

&

Luke trudged off the playing field. The Creekwood guys scored another two points. It looked like they'd win this game.

He scanned the stands for Melody, but didn't see her. Curiosity and disappointment caused his shoulders to sag. She didn't leave, did she?

When Luke reached the bench, both Jamie and Sarah were barraging Keith with questions and accusations. The terseness in the voices caused Luke to experience one of those proverbial *sinking feelings*.

"What's going on?" He almost didn't want to know, but he could guess: Keith and his picture phone. . .

"Luke, Mel's really upset," Sarah told him. "I don't know what this knucklehead said to her—"

"Hey!" An indignant frown furrowed Keith's dark brows.

"Let me repeat—we don't know what this knucklehead said, but Mel left looking really stressed."

"Totally stressed," Jamie agreed. "I've never seen her like that."

Luke stared at Keith who squirmed beneath his scrutiny. "Give me that phone."

"What?"

Luke held out his hand, and Keith reluctantly slapped the device into his palm. Flipping it open, Luke set about deleting the infamous photo, which was obviously the cause of Melody's grief.

"I'm trying to reach Mel on her cell," Sarah announced.

"She won't answer until she's calmed down." Luke realized Keith's phone wasn't all that different from his own and soon figured out how to operate it.

"She drives like a lunatic when she's upset."

Luke glanced at Jamie. "She promised me she wouldn't do that anymore." He fiddled with a few keys and searched through several files.

"I'll try her at home," Sarah said.

"Don't bother." Luke didn't think she'd seek refuge at her folks' place. He hoped Melody was at his house.

He found and removed the offensive picture from Keith's phone. Then he tossed it back and gave him what he hoped was a withering glare.

"The game's as good as over. I'll catch up to Melody. You two just pray, all right?" He glanced at Sarah then Jamie.

Both women nodded.

"And you," he said to Keith, "better keep your mouth shut."

Keith raised his hands in surrender. "Look, buddy, I'm sorry," he said with an earnest expression. "I was just trying to help."

Luke didn't reply, but collected his gear and strode to his Durango. He prayed Melody would keep her promise and wouldn't drive off like a "lunatic," as Jamie described it.

Lord, let me be her hero again, he prayed as he drove home. *This time I won't leave any questions or doubts in her mind. This time. . .* Luke paused to gather his resolve. *This time I'll tell her that I love her.*

twenty

Melody heard Luke enter the side door and walk into the kitchen, but she stayed riveted to the leather-upholstered sofa in his living room. Lexi, however, bounded through the dining room to greet him. Mel listened as Luke calmly instructed the puppy to "stay down," and "don't jump," and she almost cracked a smile.

Almost.

Had Keith shown Luke the iniquitous cell phone snapshot? Luke's voice sounded composed. What if he didn't know about it yet?

Well, it would only be a matter of time. But would he, like everyone else, believe she was capable of the same treachery that Keith accused her of?

Luke strode into the room and Mel turned to watch his approach. He didn't look angry, but his expression was hard to gauge. Concerned? Confused?

He walked toward her then paused long enough to push aside the magazines on the coffee table before he sat on it, facing her. The fabric of his blue jeans rubbed across her knees.

Melody searched his face, but didn't know where to begin. She wanted to tell him everything, but how much did he already know? What did he believe?

Fat tears filled her eyes and obstructed her vision. She put her face in her hands. Life seemed so totally hopeless.

"Mellie." Luke whispered her name and pressed his forehead against hers. He rubbed his palms up and down her bare arms. "Why are you crying?"

"Because I never want to hurt or disappoint you."

"You've done neither. So what's the problem?"

She glanced up at him and tried not to wince. "Keith didn't talk to you?"

"Oh, he talked to me, all right. He showed me the picture he took of you and Ramsay."

Mel felt sick. "Well, it's not like it seems."

"I figured."

She tried to defend herself. "I tried to call you twice today—"

"Look at me." Luke put his hands on either side of her face, forcing her gaze to meet his. "I love you, Melody. I think I've loved you since we were ten. I'm not about to believe hearsay—or even a photograph—over you." His thumb brushed the top of her upper lip.

She blinked. "You said you love me?"

Luke momentarily closed his eyes. "Oh, Melody, isn't it obvious?"

"Well, yes, but. . ." Her doom and gloom fled. She couldn't stifle a giggle. She felt almost giddy. "I love you, too, Luke. I don't know exactly when it happened, but it did." She covered his wrists with her hands. "And what I feel for you, I never felt for Scott or any other guy. It's the real thing. I know it."

His eyes grew teary. "Melody."

"It's true, Luke. I love you with all my heart."

He drew her forward and placed a sweet, undemanding kiss on her lips that left her longing for another.

"I promised your father I'd be a gentleman at all times." Luke touched his nose to hers.

"What did you promise that for?"

Luke sat back, his hands capturing hers, and wagged his head in feigned exasperation.

She grinned. "All kidding aside, I'd like nothing better than for you to kiss me for the next three hours. But I know it wouldn't be right. And as much as I never want to sadden or disappoint you, I especially don't want to disappoint the Lord

Jesus." Past mistakes scampered across her mind. "Not again."

"I want our relationship to glorify God, too." Luke glanced down at their entwined fingers then looked back at her. "Will you marry me?"

"In a heartbeat."

He sat up a little straighter. "Really?"

She grinned at his amazed expression. "Really."

"You just made my day—my year—my whole life!"

Melody's smile grew, and she saw the love he felt for her shining in his honey-brown eyes. She'd finally be a bride—and marry the man she loved so deeply.

"Oh, but—um, Luke? You'd better talk to my dad."

"I already stated my intentions. He knows."

"When did you do that?" Melody frowned—and then another piece of the puzzle fell into place. She sucked in a breath. "Wait. It was that Saturday morning in the garage, wasn't it? The day you brought Lexi home. . ."

Luke arched a dark brow and grinned. "Very good, Mystery Girl, you finally figured it out."

She laughed and gazed at their clasped hands. But, moments later, she realized it was much too quiet.

"Hey, speaking of Lexi. . ." Mel scanned the area. "Where is she?"

"In her crate." An expression of chagrin wafted across Luke's face. "I didn't want her kissing you because *I* wanted to kiss you."

They shared a chuckle.

Luke stood and dropped down onto the couch next to Melody. "Okay, want to tell me what happened today?"

"Yeah." Mel turned and tucked one leg under her, sitting sideways on the sofa.

The whole lunchtime fiasco tumbled from her lips. She told Luke every detail. When she finished, despair reared its ugly head once more.

"What am I going to do?"

Luke stared straight ahead, his mouth pursed in a thoughtful manner. Then, finally, he looked at her. "You're going to tell the truth." He stood. "Right now."

He held his hand out to her and Mel took it. Luke helped her to her feet.

"What do you mean 'right now'?"

"As in *right now*. We're going next door so you can tell your family exactly what you just told me."

Mel pulled her hand free. "Are you nuts?"

"Look, I'll help you every step of the way." Luke put his hands on his hips. "But if you don't say anything, you run the risk of being accused for not sounding the alarm in time for Bonnie to do something."

Mel didn't get it. "What do you mean? What can she do?"

"You said Ramsay's leaving tomorrow, right?"

"Yeah."

Luke glanced at his wristwatch. "It's just after ten. The night is young."

He took her hand and Mel allowed him to lead her through the house, toward the door. She prayed he was right. Luke had always been a commonsense sort of guy.

"Oh, one more thing. . ."

He stopped so fast that Mel almost tripped over his heel.

"Let's not say anything just yet about the two of us getting married. If it's okay with you, I'd like to wait a few days until I can put an engagement ring on your finger."

His words touched Mel to the core. "All right. It's our secret until then."

But as they walked hand in hand around the yards, Mel's heart broke for her sister. Bonnie never did get an engagement ring, and now she'd be deprived of the wedding that she and Mom had been planning for months.

Anxiety snaked its way around her midsection. "Luke, I don't think I can do this. What if my family doesn't believe me?"

He paused. "Then they don't believe you, and we'll deal with whatever happens next. All you can do, Melody, is tell them the truth in love. You're not responsible for their reactions."

He rang the doorbell then smacked his forehead. "Duh. You can walk right into your own home."

"Yeah, they haven't changed the locks yet."

Hearing Luke's rumble of laughter caused her to smile and relax a bit.

They entered the house and Mel willed herself to stay calm. She prayed for wisdom to "tell the truth in love," as Luke put it.

Dad sat in his recliner in the den, wearing sweatpants and a navy blue T-shirt. "Well, hi, you two." Lifting the remote, he turned off the TV. He reached for the handle on the side of chair and positioned it upright. Then he stood. "Where have you been?"

"Luke played baseball tonight. He's on the church's team."

"So I see by his T-shirt." Dad grinned at him. "Good for you."

"Thanks, Bill." Luke shook his proffered hand. "Unfortunately, we lost."

"Ya win some, ya lose some."

Mel watched as her father gave Luke a friendly slap between the shoulder blades.

"Where are Mom and Bonnie?"

"Shopping, as usual. I'm going to be broke by the time Bonnie gets hitched."

Mel tried not to grimace as she slid her hands into the pockets of her shorts. She looked up into her dad's suntanned, age-lined face. "Could I talk to you before they get home?" She glanced at Luke. "Maybe it's better we tell my father first."

He inclined his head.

"This sounds serious." Dad sat back down in his recliner.

"It is." She and Luke took a seat on the striped cover of the daybed.

She felt less intimidated talking to her dad and, after a rocky beginning, Mel spilled the whole story.

Dad sat forward. "You gotta be kidding me. He told *you* to tell Bonnie that he can't marry her?"

Mel bobbed her head, feeling like she might cry. Luke slipped his arm around her shoulders.

"What a rotten thing to do to." Dad clenched his jaw. "Scott's aware there's been strife between you two girls. He had to know this sort of thing could ruin your relationship with your sister—maybe forever."

"I don't think Scott really cares."

"Obviously."

The sound of the side door opening signaled Mom's and Bonnie's return. Shopping bags rustled, and Bonnie's laughter accompanied their entrance into the dining room where they set their purchases down on the table with a *thud*.

"I'll tell them." Dad rose then left the den. He closed the door behind him.

Mel leaned against Luke, wondering what would happen next.

"Let's pray."

Luke took her hand, and Mel fought against all the angst in her spirit long enough to follow his petition to their heavenly Father.

Minutes later, Melody's mother entered the room. Her expression was one of shock. "I can't believe it," she murmured, lowering herself onto the wooden desk chair across from the daybed. "And, of course, Bonnie won't believe it until she sees it—or hears it from Scott's mouth. She and your father are on their way over to his place right now."

"So you think I'm a liar?"

Luke squeezed her hand. "No, Melody, don't you see? It's good that Bonnie is checking things out for herself—and it's doubly good that your dad's going with her."

Melody stared at him, a frown pulling at her brows.

He explained. "If Amber said you decided not to marry me, you'd best believe I would want to discuss the matter with you *up close and personal*."

Melody's defensiveness crumbled, and she laughed. At this rate, Luke would blow their secret before she ever did.

"Luke, you're a marvelous mediator," Mom told him, sending Melody a look of warning. "And this whole thing with Scott. . . Well, it's got to be some horrible misunderstanding."

Mel wanted to shout at her mother and say that she and Bonnie were so caught up in wedding plans they wouldn't know the truth if they crashed into it with their shopping carts! But the pressure Luke applied to her hand once more kept her angry words at bay.

Minutes passed. Mom left the room, and Melody could hear her putting dishes away in the kitchen. Luke flipped on the television and occupied himself with his favorite cable news program. Soon more than an hour had gone by.

At long last Bonnie and Dad returned home, and Melody made her way into the kitchen to meet them. Luke trailed in behind her. But Bonnie ran up the stairs to their bedroom without saying a word, so Mel assumed she'd discovered the truth for herself.

With a grim expression, their father confirmed it.

"We found Scott at home, all right. But he was there with his *other* fiancée who happens to be a few months pregnant. Well, maybe more than a few. It's quite obvious the woman's expecting."

"What!" Mel gaped at her dad. She'd know all along what a creep Scott was, but she never imagined he was that much of a scoundrel!

On second thought, maybe she did.

Mel glanced at her mother, who paled at the news.

"We didn't discuss anything in front of the expectant mother, who can't be any older than Bonnie," Dad went on. "And Scott tried to dance around answering my questions, but finally he confessed to everything. It's true he's leaving for medical school tomorrow. He's breaking it off with Bonnie, but he's not taking the other girl with him, so my guess is he's running out on her, too." Dad exhaled a weary sigh. "I feel bad for her, but my first concern is Bonnie."

"He actually told Bonnie he was—was calling off the wedding?" Mom's voice sounded strained.

"Yep. 'Course I had to threaten him within an inch of his life, but—"

"Oh, Bill, this is no time for hyperbole."

"Honey, I'm not kidding. I'm a little ashamed over how I lost my temper with Scott, but no one messes with my daughters and gets away with it!"

Mel's gaze flitted from one parent to the other before settling on Luke who stood beside her.

"Luke's already been fairly warned."

He gave Dad a nod before sending Mel an affectionate wink.

"I'm sure Bonnie's devastated," Mom remarked.

Melody turned and saw tears in her mother's eyes. She could well imagine how hurt Bonnie must be.

"I suppose I should go up there and comfort her, but I know I'll just end up sobbing right along with her." Mom swatted at the moisture trickling down her cheeks. "Scott seemed so—so perfect."

"Perfect?" Mel couldn't keep silent a moment more. "Mom, how can you allow yourself to be so ignorant? Scott has been a major instigator, wreaking havoc between Bonnie and me. He's stirred up all kinds of trouble in our career group. I tried to warn all of you, but no one would listen. You thought I was the hateful one, and I've been miserable for the last few months. If it weren't for Luke, I would have probably flung myself off some cliff."

"She's right," Luke said. "Well, not about the cliff part." Stepping behind her, he placed his hands on Mel's shoulders and gave her a shake.

She nearly grinned.

"But Melody did sound the alarm more than once."

"I know she did," Dad said.

Mel saw the remorse in her father's eyes.

"She wanted to do something to prevent this very thing from happening," Luke added, "except each time she stepped in, things backfired."

"I should have listened," Dad admitted, "but, you know, as Christians, we want to forgive a person's past and move on." He looked at Melody. "Your mother and I decided Scott made his mistakes, and you made yours, and since God forgave the both of you, so should we."

"Scott never changed," Mel said, lifting a defiant chin and folding her arms.

"Yeah, well. . ." Her dad ran a hand over his bald head. "I guess we all found that out the hard way."

Mom crossed the room and gathered Melody in an embrace. "I'm so sorry you've been hurting all this time and I couldn't see it." She began to sob. "I'm so sorry, Mellie."

Mel's stony façade disintegrated. In seconds, she returned her mother's hug while tears dribbled down her own cheeks.

It was then—and only then—that Melody sensed she'd gotten her family back.

❧

Just look at those stars."

Her hand in Luke's as they strolled toward the alley, Melody lifted exhausted eyes and gazed at the sky. "It looks like black velvet with pinholes."

"No, no, you're supposed to say they look like diamonds—as in engagement rings."

Mel laughed. "Oh, right." She was so tired, she felt punchy.

The time was somewhere after three in the morning, and she already knew she'd have to call in to work. But she rarely missed a day, so her supervisor would understand, considering the circumstances. Fortunately, Bonnie seemed to be coping with Scott's rejection amazingly well—now that the initial shock had worn off.

They reached the end of the walk.

"I'll wait here and watch so you get back inside safely."

"Then who's going to watch you get in safely?"

"Melody." Luke's gentle reprimand hung between them.

She tipped her head and regarded him beneath the bright beam of the streetlamp. "You know, you're really hunky with that five o'clock shadow."

Luke rubbed the side of his face. "Would that be a five a.m. shadow?"

"I guess so." She giggled.

He gave her a sweet grin then lifted her hand. "Good night, Princess Melody," he said, placing a kiss on her fingers.

An electric current zinged up her arm. "Good night, Sir Luke. You're my knight in shining armor."

"That's because I love you."

"I know." Melody smiled. Her heart swelled with joy. "I love you, too."

epilogue

Sunshine spilled through the autumn treetops as Melody held Luke's hands while he recited his vows. Standing beneath the leafy canopy, she never felt more beautiful dressed in her white satin, short-sleeved, off the shoulder gown with its beaded lace appliqués. Melody had never imagined she'd agree to an outdoor wedding ceremony, but when Luke's sister, Amber, and her husband, Karl, offered the use of a pretty corner of their property—the spot right beside a little creek—Mel couldn't refuse. She knew it'd be perfect.

". . .to have and to hold, from this day forward, as long as we both shall live."

Luke gazed into her eyes and gave her fingers a meaningful squeeze.

She smiled.

Then it was Melody's turn. As the pastor led her, she promised to "love, honor, and cherish."

When the vows were finished, Bonnie, Mel's maid of honor, read from 1 Corinthians 13: "Love is patient, love is kind. It does not envy, it does not boast, it is not proud. It is not rude, it is not self-seeking, it is not easily angered, it keeps no record of wrongs. Love does not delight in evil but rejoices with the truth. It always protects, always trusts, always hopes, always perseveres. Love never fails."

Tears gathered in Melody's eyes. This was the first time Bonnie made it through the reading without breaking down and sobbing. But she had insisted that she wanted to read this passage. Bonnie claimed she wanted this portion of God's Word etched upon her soul forever.

Mel knew her younger sister's wounds were still raw. It had

only been four months since Scott left. Bonnie now clearly saw how wrong she had been to trust and believe him over Melody. He'd baited Bonnie with his charm, good looks, and empty promises, and she'd fallen for it hook, line, and sinker. She'd let the idea of getting married and having a home and family outweigh her common sense—as well as warnings from others, particularly her older sister. But Melody could well understand how it happened and all was forgiven. She and Bon-bon had renewed their close relationship.

And then there was Cassidy Chambers, Scott's pregnant "fiancée." After Scott's departure, Melody and her family felt God leading them to help the young woman any way possible. They reached out to her, and Cassidy allowed them to take her in under the protective wings of their friendship. Several weeks ago, they all rejoiced when she accepted the Lord Jesus Christ as her Savior and in just another month her baby would be born. As for Scott, no one knew where he'd vanished to. Bonnie did some digging and, not surprisingly, the Mayo Medical School had never heard of him.

"I now pronounce you man and wife," the pastor said. "Luke, you may kiss your bride."

Flutters of anticipation filled Melody's insides. She'd dreamed of this moment. After their initial kiss, they hadn't shared another until now.

Luke drew her into his arms and pressed his lips to hers in a way that made Mel's knees threaten to give way.

Their guests applauded.

Afterward, friends and family members tossed birdseed as Melody and Luke made their way toward the white canvas tent. Beneath its billows, the bridal party formed a queue so they could greet everyone who entered the makeshift reception area for food, wedding cake, and punch. True, it wasn't the pricey wedding Melody had always fantasized about, but she felt dizzy with happiness nonetheless.

"I love you, Melody," Luke whispered close to her ear.

She smiled. He told her that at least twenty-five times a day. "I love you, too, but those words can't come close to comparing to how I feel right now." She looped her arm around his. "I guess I'll just have to take the rest of our lives to show you how much I love you."

"I'll look forward to it." He kissed her again.

"All right, that's enough." Jamie Becker appeared wearing a black dress with white and yellow daisies and a matching yellow knit jacket. "No smooching while the guests are trying to congratulate you, okay?"

The sparkle in Jamie's brown eyes let Mel know she was teasing. Next Jamie hugged both her and Luke.

Then Keith came through the receiving line. They had long since patched things up, and now Keith was one of the most loyal friends that she and Luke knew. The entire career group, in fact, had experienced something of a spiritual revival. Gone were those days of gossiping and repeating negative things about others. Instead, every member of the group vowed to adhere to the Golden Rule.

Keith grinned at Mel before giving her a crushing bear hug. "I'm so happy for you two."

"Thanks," Luke said as he and Keith clasped hands.

After Keith sauntered off, Luke whispered to Melody, "That guy's bachelor days are numbered. I have a hunch that he and Marlene will be tying the knot soon."

Mel smiled and nodded. She thought the same thing.

"And, Melody. . ."

She stared up into her new husband's gaze. Luke kissed her once more.

"No matter how old we get, I'll always see you the way you look today. You'll always be my beautiful, blushing bride."

Her eyes filled with unshed joy. Life couldn't get any better than this.

Then again, she reminded herself that with God all things are possible!

A Letter To Our Readers

Dear Reader:

In order that we might better contribute to your reading enjoyment, we would appreciate your taking a few minutes to respond to the following questions. We welcome your comments and read each form and letter we receive. When completed, please return to the following:

Fiction Editor
Heartsong Presents
PO Box 719
Uhrichsville, Ohio 44683

1. Did you enjoy reading *Always a Bridesmaid* by Andrea Boeshaar?
   ❑ Very much! I would like to see more books by this author!
   ❑ Moderately. I would have enjoyed it more if

   _____

   _____

   _____

2. Are you a member of **Heartsong Presents**?   ❑ Yes   ❑ No
   If no, where did you purchase this book? _____

   _____

3. How would you rate, on a scale from 1 (poor) to 5 (superior), the cover design? _____

4. On a scale from 1 (poor) to 10 (superior), please rate the following elements.

   ____ Heroine   ____ Plot
   ____ Hero   ____ Inspirational theme
   ____ Setting   ____ Secondary characters

5. These characters were special because? _____

_____

_____

6. How has this book inspired your life? _____

_____

_____

7. What settings would you like to see covered in future
   Heartsong Presents books? _____

_____

_____

8. What are some inspirational themes you would like to see
   treated in future books? _____

_____

_____

9. Would you be interested in reading other **Heartsong
   Presents** titles? ❏ Yes ❏ No

10. Please check your age range:
   ❏ Under 18   ❏ 18-24
   ❏ 25-34   ❏ 35-45
   ❏ 46-55   ❏ Over 55

Name _____

Occupation _____

Address _____

City, State, Zip_____

fresh-brewed love

4 stories in 1

four women find grounds for love in these well-blended novellas. JJ is determined to make a success of her business no matter what. Kasey is the hapless victim of a matchmaking scheme. Kae fears her remaining days will be spent under the shadow of an old friendship. Carrie's desire to cover the story of a lifetime may overshadow any chances of future happiness. Can these women make the right decisions when it comes to love?

Contemporary, paperback, 352 pages, 5³⁄₁₆" x 8"

Please send me _____ copies of *Fresh-Brewed Love*. I am enclosing $6.97 for each.
(Please add $2.00 to cover postage and handling per order. OH add 7% tax.)

Send check or money order, no cash or C.O.D.s, please.

Name_____

Address _____

City, State, Zip _____

To place a credit card order, call 1-740-922-7280.
Send to: Heartsong Presents Readers' Service, PO Box 721, Uhrichsville, OH 44683

Presents